"Are you Miss Katherine Wallace?"

Her eyes remained wide as she nodded. "How did you know. . . ?"

He gave her an apologetic smile as he removed his hat. "My aunt mentioned you in her letter. I'm very sorry I frightened you."

"That's quite all right, Major Kirby. I'm. . .very glad you're home safe. Mary's. . .been so terribly worried."

He frowned and regretted he hadn't at least sent them a telegram before he left. "I'm afraid I received Aunt Mary's letter right as the siege at Petersburg ended. There was very little time to do anything. Then General Lee surrendered. . . ."

"Of course! I. . .I understand perfectly, Major Kirby." Although her voice shook, it was gentle and reassuring. "And I'm sure Mary will as well."

Daniel looked at her curiously. She had to be one of the very few daughters of the Confederacy he had met who had not instantly hated him on sight. A Southern woman's zeal for the cause was almost legendary. He had been spit on, snubbed, and bad-mouthed any number of times. And unlike other young ladies he'd met, Northern or Southern, she made no attempt to flirt with him. In fact, judging by the way she stumbled over her words, she seemed painfully shy.

JENNIFER A. DAVIDS has lived in Ohio all her life, and her family are longtime residents of the state. Her mother's side of the family is from central and southern Ohio, and her father has traced his side of the family tree back to the early eighteen hundreds. She is a graduate of Ohio State University and feels blessed to have been called to a life of writing for the Lord. She lives in central Ohio with her husband and two children and sings on the praise team at church. If she's not writing, she's reading, crafting, or watching a favorite movie or TV show—usually in that order!

Yankee Heart

Jennifer A. Davids

Blessings!
Math 5:16

[signature]

Heartsong Presents

I would like to thank the Ohio Historical Society, Slate Run Living Historical Farm, and the Columbus Metropolitan Library for helping me with all the historical information needed to write this book. Many thanks to my husband, Doug, our two children, Jonathan and Grace, my extended family, and my church family for supporting me as a writer. And last but never least, a great deal of thanks to My Father in Heaven. Thank You for giving me the honor of being Your scribe.

This book is lovingly dedicated to my Grandma Minnie and my Great Aunt Jennie. You both were Ohio to me and are dearly missed.

A note from the Author:
I love to hear from my readers! You may correspond with me by writing:

Jennifer A. Davids
Author Relations
PO Box 721
Uhrichsville, OH 44683

ISBN 978-1-61626-362-1

YANKEE HEART

All scripture quotations are taken from the King James Version of the Bible.

Our mission is to publish and distribute inspirational products offering exceptional value and biblical encouragement to the masses.

PRINTED IN THE U.S.A.

one

Katherine Eliza Wallace looked around her with wide eyes as she stepped off the train. Rising over the top of the tiny railway station were the false fronts of buildings, their painted signs announcing the Ostrander Hotel and Decker's Dry Goods. Yet another store advertised furniture notions to her left. But it wasn't the sight of the simple country shops that caused her to stare. A light snow was falling, the first the South Carolinian had seen in the twenty-two years of her life.

Her companion watched her with a gentle smile. "I've missed snow," she said as she also watched the tiny flecks of icy softness swirl through the air.

Katherine turned to look at the woman, slightly embarrassed. "It's lovely," she declared in her soft Southern drawl. Then she shivered in spite of her warm wraps. "But my, it's chilly!"

The older woman chuckled. "It'll be spring in a couple of weeks. I warned you it would be different than living along the Congaree."

"I don't mind." Katherine's face grew pensive. "You know I had nowhere else to turn."

Mary grasped her hand. "Welcome to Ohio," she said with a grin. "Ten to one it'll be warmer tomorrow and then freezing the day after." They laughed.

A shrill cry rang out and they turned toward it. "Mary O'Neal!" A graying, scarecrow-like woman was bearing down on them from the direction of the dry goods store.

Katherine looked at Mary nervously.

The older woman smiled reassuringly and smoothed back a strand of Katherine's dark hair, tucking it back into her bonnet. "It'll be fine," she whispered and turned to the new woman's outstretched arms. "Ruth Decker!" Mary smiled as she gently returned the strong embrace. "It's so good to be home."

Grasping her friend by the elbows, Ruth smiled back as she examined Mary's face.

"We thought you might be here soon. I'm so glad. We heard about General Sherman's march. The *Delaware Gazette* said he went right through where your plantation stood." She drew a little closer to Mary. "Did the general. . .burn your house down?" She finished the last sentence in a sort of loud whisper.

"No, he was very good to us while he and his officers stayed at the house."

Ruth gasped and her eyes became so large Katherine thought they looked just like those of the tree frogs that were so common in her home state.

"Mary O'Neal," she gasped. The train began to leave and her voice rose above the laboring engine. "You met General William Tecumseh Sherman and didn't tell me straightaway!" She picked up one of the carpetbags Mary had set down on the platform. "Now you just come with me and tell me everything!" Mary gave Katherine a droll little smile and they picked up their other bags and followed.

With the train gone Katherine got a glimpse of the rest of the town. The tall spire of a church rose up further down, and across the street and a block or so closer was a brick schoolhouse. Several other homes dotted the rest of the town, and in the distance she heard the distinct sounds of bleating sheep.

"A purebred sheep dealer a street or two over," Mary explained.

They stepped up onto the wooden boardwalk outside the dry goods store, and Katherine noticed there was a post office just around the corner. Evidently it was also taken care of by the Deckers, for Ruth stuck her head in as they passed to tell her daughter, a young lady named May, to mind the counter; she would be "back in a bit."

The walkway ended at a stone-lined path at the end of which stood a quaint whitewashed two-story house. Quicker than a body could say "knife" Ruth Decker had them out of their wraps and sitting in her elegant little parlor sipping tea out of a china service she claimed her grandmother had brought over from Ireland.

"Now," Ruth said as she came into the room with a plate of cookies, "tell me everything." She sat down next to Mary and took her hand.

Mary smiled gently at her friend. "If you don't mind, Ruth, first I would like to introduce you to my dear friend, Katherine Wallace."

"Good heavens, where are my manners!" Ruth leaned over and patted Katherine on the leg. "I am so sorry, dear. I was caught up with seeing Mary again."

"Please don't give it another thought, ma'am," Katherine said softly. "I'm pleased to make your acquaintance."

Ruth started at the sound of the young woman's gentle accent and looked at Mary.

"Katherine's family owned the plantation next to ours, Ruth." Mary calmly took a sip of tea. "The Wallaces. I'm sure I wrote you about them."

Ruth looked at Katherine a moment longer. "Oh of course. Yes. How do you do?"

Katherine noted the cooler tone to the woman's voice and flushed slightly as she took another sip of tea. It wasn't the first time since they had passed the Mason-Dixon Line that she had been snubbed in such a way. But it hurt just the same. She lightly fingered the long, thin scar that lined her left jawline.

"For man looketh on the outward appearance, but the Lord looketh on the heart."

The verse sprang into her mind of its own volition, and Katherine remembered it as one Mary had quoted after a particularly bad incident in Springfield, west of Ostrander. Katherine felt her face cool a little and, dropping her hand away from her jaw, took mind of Mary and Ruth's conversation.

"You mean General Sherman used your house as his headquarters!" Ruth was gushing.

Mary smiled. "Well, not exactly. He and his staff simply stayed the evening. We gave him what we could, and he provided Katherine and me with a horse and wagon, which got us up to Lexington. There was no catching a train so far south. He'd ruined the lines."

The tree frog eyes appeared once more. "You traveled from South Carolina to Lexington, Kentucky, all by yourself! Mary O'Neal, wasn't it dangerous?"

"No." Katherine spoke now with a soft voice. "There are many refugees on the roads these days. We had a great deal of company on our way here." She looked at Mary. "I'm afraid General Sherman has made many a family homeless."

Ruth gave her a sharp look and then turned to Mary. "What is the general like?"

"He's a bit rough, but he's a good man," Mary said with a sympathetic glance at Katherine.

When Sherman's army had arrived at her family's plantation, they destroyed everything, including burning the house to the ground. Katherine and her aunt Ada had fled to the O'Neals', whose plantation was mostly spared when General Sherman discovered it housed a fellow Ohioan. Her aunt had been quite indignant over that fact, but Katherine had been very glad her friend's home had been spared.

"My people were so happy to see him," she said. "He remarked that many former slaves clamor around him as if he were Moses."

Ruth looked at her friend with reproof. "I still can't believe you and John actually owned slaves. How could you, coming from a family like yours? Your people have been abolitionists for years."

Mary patted Ruth's hand. "Well, you know my husband's inheriting the place was quite a surprise to us. We had intended on freeing our people and selling the land, but a stipulation in the will demanded the plantation couldn't be broken up. It would have been given over to a distant cousin we knew to be terribly cruel. So we thought it best to keep it." Mary smiled at Ruth. "We were kind to our people and kept them well cared for."

"And you were the least popular family for it." Katherine smiled broadly. "Folks said they would turn on you because of your kindness."

Ignoring Katherine's comment, Ruth clasped Mary's hand once more. "Dorothy told us about John and Thomas. We're so sorry."

Katherine looked compassionately at her friend. The mention of the loss of Mary's husband and son had brought a strained look to her face. Her husband, John O'Neal, and their son, Thomas, had sneaked north and joined the Union army not long after the surrender of Fort Sumter. John had been with a Pennsylvania regiment and Thomas with one from New York State. Thomas had perished at Chancellorsville; John only two months later at Gettysburg. With her son and husband gone, Mary had longed for family and decided to abandon her plantation and return to Ohio where her sister, Dorothy, lived along with her three sons. Dorothy's husband had died before the war, and other relatives had either gone west or passed on.

Katherine frowned as Ruth prattled on about who else in Ostrander had lost loved ones in the war. Couldn't she see how tired Mary was and how sad the news made her? When the woman finally paused to draw breath, Katherine spoke up. "Shouldn't we be getting along to your sister's farm, Mary? You said you wanted to go there directly, seeing how it's been so long since you had a letter." Mary shot her a grateful glance.

"Oh of course," Ruth exclaimed. "I've been keeping you! I'm so glad you're on your way to Dolly's. It's been at least two weeks since I've seen her here in town."

"Two weeks?" Mary immediately rose and made for their wraps which hung on an oak hall tree near the door.

Katherine followed her lead.

"Well yes. Elijah Carr was coming to get her mail—"

"Mr. Carr has been coming to town for my sister?" Katherine started at the stern look on Mary's face as she handed her things to her.

"Well yes, to get the mail and buy a few things." Ruth looked in wonder at Mary's confused look. "Toby ran off and joined up nearly two years ago. With Jonah and Daniel gone fighting, she needed the help."

Mary paled and leaned back against the door.

Katherine thought she might faint and grasped her arm.

"Oh Mary, I'm so sorry!" Ruth exclaimed. "I thought you knew! I was sure she'd written—"

"Hush up!" Katherine snapped. Seeing Mary so distressed made her sharp. Ruth stopped her chatter, but Katherine could feel her eyes on her as she began to rub Mary's wrists. "Mary, are you well?"

Taking a deep breath, the older woman nodded. "May we borrow your horse and buggy, Ruth? I need to see my sister."

"Of course!"

৶

At least the woman is efficient, Katherine thought as she tooled a little black buggy down the road out of town.

It hadn't taken Ruth Decker long to get them going. She had even offered to get a boy to drive them, but Katherine had insisted on performing the task to the woman's great surprise; she hadn't seemed to believe her capable. *Two weeks ago she would have been right,* the young woman mused.

The trip up from the South had forced Katherine to learn and do things she had never done in the whole of her privileged life—like driving a horse and wagon and cooking over an open flame. She was glad to have learned them. She'd never felt very comfortable having others do things for her or being prim and proper as was expected of a Southern belle. She was glad she was becoming more self-sufficient, particularly now.

Ruth had given Mary her sister's mail for the last two weeks, and she knew Mary would want to look at the correspondence in private, meager though it was. There were a grand total of three letters in the bundle, two of them from Daniel, one of Dorothy's sons, and one from someone whose name Mary hadn't recognized. Katherine had noted it was from a Union officer and hoped it wasn't bad news. She wasn't sure how much more Mary could take today. Her friend now flipped through the letters one at a time, her steel blue eyes pensive and a loose strand of ash blond hair tickling her face, trying in vain to gain her attention.

"Maybe you should open one," Katherine suggested softly.

Mary glanced at her and looked as if she might refuse.

"I'm sure your sister wouldn't mind."

Biting her lip, Mary opened one of Daniel's, the most recent one. "He's in Petersburg, Virginia, with General Grant." She breathed a small sigh of relief. "He says homesickness is all he's come down with in the last month."

Katherine nodded and sent up a prayer of thankfulness. Sickness was such a problem in the army camps of both sides, it was feared almost as much as combat.

Mary looked at the other letter from the unknown Union officer. "This is dated before Daniel's," she muttered. She turned weary eyes to Katherine. "It may be about Jonah. . . . I. . .can't. . ." She raised a hand to her eyes.

"Then don't," Katherine said. "You're so tired. . .I regret suggesting it."

Mary tucked the missives in her reticule and looked around. The familiar scenery seemed to soothe her, and Katherine sensed her tension ease and a little of her weariness fall away.

The road they traveled down had trees thick on both sides and every now and then a squirrel, not long from a winter nap, dashed in and out of the leaves. The snow had not lasted long at all, having only served to make a light coating on bare patches of grass and frost the sides of the road.

When they rolled past a neatly kept brick church, Mary mentioned that was where her family had attended since before there was even a building to meet in. She sincerely hoped Katherine would enjoy Mill Creek Church.

Katherine bit her lip and glanced out away from Mary's eye. *I know I'll enjoy it, but will the church enjoy me?*

She thought back over their visit with Mrs. Decker. Were people like Ruth Decker the kind of folk she had to look forward to? In spite of the woman's chilly behavior, she regretted being so sharp right before they left. And comparing the poor woman to a tree frog! She felt the color rise slightly in her cheeks. *I ought to be ashamed of myself.*

Katherine was hoping to start a new life here, far, far away from the one she had left behind in South Carolina. Ohio was to be her home now.

I surely got off on the wrong foot with Mrs. Decker, Father. Help me to behave better the next time we meet.

"My, but Mill Creek is high."

Katherine started at the sound of Mary's voice. She had been so lost in thought she had not noticed a rushing sound that was quickly becoming a roar. They were approaching a creek—Mill Creek, according to Mary.

Katherine stopped the horse for a moment to look. The creek was a tumult of rushing water running quickly past them as if on serious business that would not wait. The spring thaw had made the waters run high and fast. It seemed slightly smaller than the Congaree, the waterway near the plantation where she grew up. But according to Mary it wasn't called Mill Creek for nothing. It powered more than one mill along its banks.

A covered bridge spanned the creek and Katherine urged the horse forward. Not long afterward they came to a crossroad and Mary instructed her to turn east. After crossing the creek once more, the trees began to thin and Katherine noticed Mary's face take on a gentle, happy look, much to her relief. The creek was on their right and the road now followed the base of a gentle slope. As they rounded a slight corner, the rear of a farmhouse came into view.

"There it is," Mary murmured.

Katherine pulled the buggy up the sloped driveway and turned to see a kindly, cozy-looking farmhouse. Painted a simple white with a slate roof, a little dormer window capped the square front porch. The pine green shutters on the windows were open and welcomed all to come in. Smoke was rising from one of the twin chimneys which rose from either side of the house, and Katherine found herself longing to sit before its fire away from the chill.

"This isn't right," she heard Mary say. "Dolly wouldn't stand for the farm to be in such a state."

Confused, Katherine turned and saw that her friend was

looking out at the scene in front of the buggy. She had been so absorbed admiring the house she hadn't noticed the rest of the farm. The yard and other farm buildings were in poor condition. More than one rail in the garden fence was broken. The barn door was standing half open, and several chickens, loose from the coop, wandered here and there.

Before she could say a word, Mary was out of the buggy and in the house.

Katherine looked around for a place to leave the horse and buggy, eager to follow. But Ruth's horse, a gentle old mare, had already raised one hoof and appeared to be dozing. She secured the brake and followed Mary into the house.

Finding herself in a little entry hall with stairs in front of her, she was unsure where to go. To the right was a charming little parlor with rose-print wallpaper, comfortable-looking chairs, and a sofa; a dining room with a long, sturdy table and chairs lay to the left. Mary was nowhere to be found.

"Katherine?"

Hearing her friend's call, Katherine immediately ascended. Halfway up she heard the worst coughing she had ever heard in her life, and the sound made her dash up the last few steps. There were several doors to choose from at the top. All were closed save one. She entered the room and nearly gasped at the sight of a woman in bed, covered with a handmade quilt. Her face was drawn and pale, and it grieved Katherine to come to the conclusion that this was Dorothy Kirby.

Mary sat on the edge of the bed trying to urge her sister to drink from a cup. "The fire's low. Go through the dining room and there should be some wood in the kitchen."

The tightness in the older woman's voice gave Katherine speed, and she flew down the stairs as directed to the kitchen in the rear of the house. The woodbox had several logs in it, and seizing a few of the thicker ones, she lugged them back upstairs. It didn't take her long to get the fire going again.

She turned to find Dorothy looking at her. She swallowed hard. It felt like a walnut with its green spring husk still attached was trying to go down her throat. Would her presence alarm the sick woman? Dorothy couldn't possibly know who she was.

She started to step out of the room when Mary motioned for her to come near.

"Pneumonia," Mary stated as she approached.

"Is that Katherine?" A catch grew in Katherine's throat at the sound of the poor woman's hoarse, weak voice.

"Yes, but hush now," Mary soothed. "We'll save introductions for later, Dolly."

But the woman shook her head. "Been praying for her. Like you asked." She made an attempt to give Katherine a weak smile but began to cough again.

"Maybe she'll quiet down if I leave." While gratified that Mary had asked her sister to pray for her, Katherine was more eager to let the woman rest.

Mary shook her head, seemingly resigned to something Katherine was unwilling to consider.

"Toby. . . ," Dolly began.

"I know. He's fighting."

Dolly shook her head and looked toward her night table.

Mary took the letter lying there and read the first few lines and then handed the letter to Katherine.

Toby had died at Cold Harbor, Virginia, a little less than a year ago.

"Jonah?" Mary's voice was barely above a whisper.

Tears smarted at Katherine's eyes as she watched Dolly shake her head.

Mary bit her lip and drew the letters from Daniel from her reticule. "Daniel's all right. He's in Petersburg."

Her sister nodded and closed her eyes. Her breathing was ragged for a minute or two. It became shallower and shallower, and Katherine gently grasped Mary's shoulder as Dorothy Kirby left to go to her reward.

Tears flowed freely down Katherine's face as she sat down on the edge of the bed and held Mary as she sobbed.

Oh Father, she prayed, *dear Mary has lost so much. Keep Daniel safe and let this sad war come to an end. Soon.*

Bootsteps sounded on the stairs and Katherine rose, standing protectively over Mary who still sat on the bed. A huge, gruff-looking man filled the doorway, and fear gripped Katherine as she saw the rifle in his hand.

But Mary knew the stranger. "Mr. Carr," she said calmly, far more calmly than Katherine thought her capable of just a few minutes after her sister's death. The older woman stood, handkerchief in hand.

Surprised, he said the name almost under his breath. "Mary O'Neal!" Clearing his throat, he took his straw hat from his head. Long strands of gray hair tumbled clumsily into his eyes and he immediately pushed them back. "Mrs. O'Neal, I—I wasn't expectin' you."

"I understood from Ruth Decker you were helping Dolly run the farm."

Mr. Carr nodded. "Yes, that's right. Since that rascal Toby took off."

"I'll thank you not to speak ill of the dead, Mr. Carr."

"Sorry," he mumbled gruffly and nodded toward the bed. "How's your sister?"

"Mrs. Kirby has passed," Mary said softly as she turned back to her sister. As she did so, Katherine thought she caught a brief gleam in Elijah Carr's eye.

"If you want to gather up a few things, I'll wait outside for you." His voice strained not to sound eager.

"What on earth for?" Mary asked suddenly, turning from her sister.

"Well. . . ," he began hesitantly. "Thing is. . .Dolly promised the farm to me."

Mary stared at him. "I'm quite sure that must be a misunderstanding. Dolly would never give up this land. Joseph always intended it for the boys."

"Jonah and Toby are gone, Mary. Died fighting the war."

"But Daniel is still alive and well, Mr. Carr." She walked up to him. He towered over her but she paid him no mind. "I read a letter from him this morning. He's with General Grant in Petersburg."

"Daniel always had a head for book learnin'. He was already an instructor over at that college of his. He was never a farmer. Dolly said with Jonah and Toby gone he would most likely sell me the land."

"Dolly said that?"

"She surely did."

Mary looked at him carefully. "Be that as it may, whether or not to sell the land to you is for Daniel to decide. And until he comes home, we'll stay right here and keep the farm going."

Katherine took a step forward to stand right behind Mary, backing up her words. She grasped the older woman's hand and squeezed it. She had no idea how to run a farm, but she was more than willing to try.

Her movement attracted Mr. Carr's attention, and he looked at Katherine as if just noticing her. "Who are you?" he asked gruffly.

With a pounding heart she raised her chin. "My name is Katherine Wallace, sir."

At the sound of her voice, Mr. Carr glared at Mary. "What do you mean bringing a filthy little secesh up here? Dolly most likely died of shock from you letting her step foot in her house."

Mary glared right back at him. Secesh, short for secessionist, was a word they had both heard spoken in anger far too often since coming north. Mary thought it a cruel name, but Katherine felt it was an accurate one.

"Miss Wallace is my dear friend and I had my sister's permission long ago to bring her here." She crossed her arms over her chest. "Dolly would have more of a fit if she could see the state the farm is in right now."

Mr. Carr looked uneasy. "Been hard," he finally muttered. "When she took ill she insisted on stayin' here. I've been goin' back and forth to take care of my lands, too."

"So you were at your farm all morning?"

Carr looked at Mary rigidly. "Had business up in Delaware this morning that wouldn't wait." His excuse that he'd had to drive nearly nine miles to the county seat clearly did not convince Mary. "She made me go," he said defensively. "Said she'd be just fine."

Mary's shoulders fell wearily. She seemed either out of arguments or too tired to continue sparring with him. She turned and sat down next to her sister's still form. "I guess I should thank you for being so neighborly after Toby left. Thank you."

Mr. Carr approached her, giving Katherine a hard look as he brushed by her.

"I'm sorry Dolly's gone. Let me take you back to my house. You could stay there a spell. . . ."

"No thank you. We have the farm to look after."

The man gritted his teeth in silent frustration.

"But if you would be so kind," Mary continued, "as to take Ruth Decker's horse and buggy back into Ostrander I would appreciate it. And please call on Rev. Warren on your way by Mill Creek Church. I need to lay my sister to rest."

Mr. Carr nodded and, without so much as a glance at

Katherine, left the room. Presently they heard the distinct sound of a wagon pulling away from the house.

"Father, forgive me for disliking that man," Mary murmured.

Katherine looked at her questioningly, but her friend said nothing more.

Instead she leaned forward and folded Dolly's arms across her waist. She then grasped the patchwork quilt and gently pulled it over her sister's body. "We'll talk later, Katherine. For now, we need to get ready for Rev. Warren."

two

Katherine tossed in her bed for what seemed like the hundredth time. In spite of all she had done and been through today, sleep refused to call on her. Too many thoughts ran through her mind.

To begin with, Mary had insisted on her using one of the unused rooms upstairs. One of her nephew's rooms. It hadn't seemed proper, but where else would she sleep? The barn? She supposed it simply felt odd to be sleeping in a man's bed. Mary had thought she would be most comfortable in Daniel's room and insisted he wouldn't mind. She would have felt much more comfortable in Dolly's room, but that would need airing out. *And besides,* she thought, *Mary should have her sister's room.*

Mr. Carr had spoken to Rev. Warren as Mary had asked, for the reverend and his wife, Minnie, soon arrived to help her with all the arrangements. They had been kind and sympathetic toward Mary, but the couple seemed to keep Katherine at a polite distance. At least they were a tad warmer than Ruth Decker.

She played with a thread in the quilt that covered her. She had kept herself busy in the kitchen while Rev. Warren spoke to Mary, and she had rounded up the loose chickens while Mary and the reverend's wife laid Dorothy out in the parlor. Making herself as scarce as possible was all she could think of to avoid the discreet coldness of the couple. In light of their behavior, alongside Ruth Decker's, she could only imagine how people would treat her at the funeral on Saturday.

She rolled over and stared at the ceiling. When she had

insisted on coming north with Mary, she had not really thought about how people would treat her. In retrospect, she realized she had latched on to the silly notion that the North was a sort of wonderland where everyone was warm and friendly and welcomed strangers with open arms. How could she help it? Mary had been the standard she had used to measure all Northerners.

The anger and suspicion Katherine aroused had come as shocking as a slap on the face. The instant any Northerner heard her voice it was assumed she was either a secessionist or worse, a Southern spy.

I was a fool to think people would assume otherwise. Mary warned me it might be this way, but I was so happy to be coming to the North. . . . Why shouldn't people be suspicious? The war certainly isn't over yet. Oh why didn't I just stay put?

She put a hand to her eyes and sighed deeply. She couldn't stay and live a life she didn't want with a family who had never wanted her.

Andrew Wallace, Katherine's father, had never forgiven her for not possessing her mother's beauty and vivaciousness. His only daughter's shy and studious spirit only irritated him. As far as he was concerned her only value to him lay in whom she married. Her brother, Charles, had always blamed her for their mother's death. Annabelle Wallace had died giving birth to her. And her father's sister, Aunt Ada, had always contended that it was downright shocking the Wallace family could have conceived a drab little nothing like Katherine.

But God opened a wide window for her when the O'Neals became the Wallaces' neighbors the year Katherine turned thirteen. John O'Neal had inherited a prosperous plantation and was connected to a very old South Carolinian family. Therefore, they immediately had standing in the community despite the fact they were Yankees.

She and Mary had become fast friends at the picnic held to welcome them, and when Katherine was sent off to school in Columbia she corresponded regularly with Mary. The older woman became the mother Katherine had always longed for. It was Mary whom she confided in, Mary who led her to a deeper relationship with Christ, Mary who had shown her the ills of slavery.

Katherine smiled sleepily. *Thank You for my dear friend, Father. Thank You for bringing us here safely. . . .* She yawned as weariness crept over her. Folks here would surely come around once they got to know her. Closing her eyes, she drifted off to sleep.

The crack of a whip shot though the air and Katherine started at the sound of it. Dropping her book, she ran through the house and into the kitchen.

The cook grabbed her as she tried to race out the back door. "Don't be goin' out there, Miss Katherine!"

"Who is it, Clarissa? Who's being whipped?"

Before the woman could answer, the crack of the whip and a scream rent the air.

Katherine pried loose and tore out of the house. She half ran, half stumbled down the slope toward the whipping post her father kept in full sight of the sad shacks which housed the Wallace slaves.

Another scream tore through her heart and Katherine suddenly realized who it was.

"Chloe," she whimpered as the post came into view. Without thought for herself or the state of mind her father was surely in, she ran to her friend and stood between the poor young slave woman and the long black whip. Her eyes rose to the man holding it, and she gasped to see it was her father and not the overseer as she had expected.

Her father swore and yanked her out of the way.

*Katherine fought but he was too strong. He shoved her into
the hands of the overseer who stood nearby, and Andrew
Wallace continued his vicious attack.*

*Katherine wailed, and when her father finally stopped
his brutality, he turned and backhanded her. Searing pain
shot through her jaw, and she soon felt blood trickling down
her neck and onto the fine French lace of her morning gown.
With a shaking hand, she reached up and touched the gash his
signet ring had made.*

*"Next time," he roared as she sobbed, "it will be someone
else tied to that post. You hear me?"*

"Katherine, do you hear me?"

Katherine awoke to find Mary sitting at the edge of her
bed, gently shaking her awake. She reached for her jaw. It was
wet. She pulled her hand away and saw not blood but tears,
which fell free and fast down her face. She looked up at her
friend. Moonlight reflected in her motherly eyes and brought
the young woman out of her nightmare.

"Chloe?" Mary asked gently.

Katherine nodded and the older woman handed her a
handkerchief.

"I'm so sorry I woke you," she said as she propped herself on
one elbow to dry her face.

"Don't worry yourself over that."

Mary smoothed Katherine's hair, tucking in loose strands
which had come loose from her long braid. "Seems like you
had that dream a number of times on our journey back."

Katherine lowered her eyes.

Mary put a finger beneath her chin and lifted her face until
their eyes met. "God knows you had no intention of doing
what you did. His Son's blood covers all sin."

"But what about Chloe? I never got to tell her how sorry. . ."

Fresh tears filled Katherine's eyes.

"I'm sure wherever she is she has forgiven you."

Katherine nodded, but even though she knew Mary was right, she still felt guilty. She had only wanted the best for Chloe, the young slave woman who had been her only friend through her lonely childhood. Teaching her how to read had been her way of setting her free. Katherine, then sixteen, hadn't really cared that it was against Southern law. Her father may have controlled the young woman's body, but Katherine knew if she was educated, at least her mind could go wherever she wished.

How could she have been so foolish as to have let her emotions get the better of her? But the things her father had said that evening at dinner. . . Even now his horrid, ugly words rolled back and forth in her mind, causing her to shake with anger. If only she had kept her tongue, Chloe would never have been beaten senseless and Katherine would have no scar to mar her face.

She sighed and looked at Mary. Chloe hadn't been the only one affected by her rash actions. "How did Thomas take it when I left?" she ventured. Her father had sent her off to Charleston for six months after the incident.

Mary hesitated. "It was hard for him."

"I'm sorry, Mary. I'm sorry I hurt your feelings. . .and Thomas's. Father said you bewitched me."

Mary said nothing, and Katherine knew she was trying not to say what she felt. She had hoped Katherine would one day truly become her daughter by marrying her son.

That had been Katherine's hope as well, but any chance she may have had with Thomas was dashed when her father forced her to break off all communication with the O'Neals. And he made arrangements to make sure it would stay that way. For the past seven years Katherine had no contact with them until the night she and her aunt were forced to find refuge with

Mary after their house had been destroyed.

"That's all water under the bridge now," Mary said finally. "I just hope your father and your brother made their peace with God before the war took their lives."

"I hope Aunt Ada does the same," Katherine said thoughtfully. "I'm going to write to her and let her know I'm safe."

"That would probably be best. Maybe you'll be able to reconcile with her."

"I'm afraid I've burned that bridge." Her aunt had disowned her when Katherine insisted on going north with Mary rather than accompanying her to Charleston. "I've never seen her so angry, not even after. . .Chloe."

Mary sighed. "Well, we should be getting back to sleep. Lots to do tomorrow." Mary rose and pulled the quilt over Katherine. Her face fell a little. "I guess we'll both be posting letters. I have to write to Daniel. He and Dolly were close."

"I'll keep him in my prayers."

Her friend gently smiled her thanks and went back to her room.

Katherine rose and in spite of the chill of the room stood in front of the window. She looked up at the moon and watched its soft light gently play on the bare trees outside her window. Sending up a quick prayer, she asked God to comfort Daniel Kirby's heart when he heard the news of his mother's passing.

As she turned to go back to bed she noticed piles of books on the floor with more stacked on a rough-hewn table. She longed to see what tomes Mary's nephew possessed, but she knew if she started looking at them now she would never get back to sleep.

She climbed into bed. *Help me sleep well, Father, so I can be a help to Mary tomorrow.* But as she laid her head back, she found herself fingering her scar. She rolled over, trying not to drown in the guilt that washed over her.

three

Appomattox Courthouse, Virginia, April 9, 1865

Confederate general Robert E. Lee stepped out the door of the borrowed farmhouse belonging to Wilmer McLean. While his horse was being rebridled, he pulled on his riding gloves and seemingly without thought plowed his fist into his other hand several times. He didn't seem to notice the numerous Union officers, who were waiting in the yard, rise respectfully at his approach. The arrival of Traveler seemed to wake him and, with great dignity, he mounted the gray horse.

At that moment, Union general Ulysses S. Grant, to whom Lee had just surrendered his forces, approached him and tipped his hat.

Major Daniel Kirby was among the officers waiting outside the house when Lee came out. He and the others around him followed Grant's example.

Lee returned the act of respect and courtesy in kind and rode off with his aide, Colonel Charles Marshall.

Daniel looked after the valiant general with sympathy. He had fought hard and bravely for his cause, and while Daniel knew that cause had been terribly wrong, he still felt such valor should be respected and honored. Gunshots, a victory salute, suddenly rang out and the twenty-five-year-old snapped his head around in consternation. *It's over, they are our countrymen again. We shouldn't humiliate them.*

It was as if General Grant had read his thoughts, for he quickly ordered all celebration to cease. He, too, saw no need to crow over their prisoners. As he turned, Daniel caught the general's eye and gave him a small nod of approval. Grant gave him a wink and the barest of smiles as he went back into the McLean house.

"Let us pray the peace in the next few months is as respectful." Daniel turned to see General Joshua Chamberlain mounted on his horse, Charlemagne, standing next to the fence.

He walked over to the general, leading his own horse, Scioto, behind him. "I know that's how the president wants it, sir."

Chamberlain nodded. "Unfortunately, not everyone up North is very pleased with the prospect." He pulled a letter from his wife out of his pocket. "Fanny writes that people are eager for reprisals, revenge."

"If there is that type of bloody work, there won't be peace for long," Daniel replied grimly.

The general nodded in agreement. They both gazed down the road General Lee had just ridden down.

" 'Rejoice not when thine enemy falleth, and let not thine heart be glad when he stumbleth,'" Daniel softly quoted.

"Amen." The general turned to look at the young major. "Have you heard from your people recently?"

Daniel looked up at the general, his face suddenly quite sober. He indeed had received word from home—an unexpected letter from his Aunt Mary. It had come just as the siege at Petersburg had ended and they had General Lee on the run. There had been no time for him to reply or even think about it until this very moment. He took the letter out now and looked at it gravely.

"What is it?" His friend's voice sounded small and far off.

"I could use some coffee," Daniel heard himself reply.

"Mount up and let's have some then," Joshua said quietly.

Putting the letter back into his pocket, Daniel mounted

Scioto and followed the general to his encampment, not far from town. They didn't speak and Daniel was glad.

Joshua always seemed to know when to speak up or remain silent. Like the time they had first met, a day or so after Fredericksburg, at the beginning of the war. It had been a horrific battle and Daniel still winced at the mere thought of it. His regiment, the 4th Ohio Infantry, had lost a shocking amount of men. The platoon he had been charged with had nearly been wiped out. Joshua, then a lieutenant colonel, had called to him as he aimlessly wandered through the army's encampment and invited him over to his campfire. Daniel had approached him warily, wondering if he was about to be reprimanded for the loss of his men. He had only been a first lieutenant at the time. But the superior officer spoke not a word about the battle and instead asked about Daniel's schooling, having heard he had graduated from Ohio Wesleyan and had taught there before the war. He asked about the university and talked about his own years as a professor of rhetoric at Bowdoin College in his home state of Maine, and their friendship began. Joshua never treated him like an underling while they were off duty, and they watched out for one another in battle. They had saved each other from certain death more than once. Daniel was proud to have such a man as a friend.

They eventually reached Joshua's tent, and Daniel soberly read his aunt Mary's letter while his friend made the coffee. When he had finished, he looked up to find Joshua seated at the small table he used to lay out military maps. Two tin mugs of coffee sat in front of him, and Daniel sat down and took a sip of the harsh brew. He looked at the general. "It's from my aunt Mary."

Joshua's brows knit together. "I thought she was in South Carolina."

Daniel shook his head. "When General Sherman went

through she made her way back up to Ohio. When she got back she found my mother dying from pneumonia."

He covered his eyes with his hand. The war was coming to a close. Death, his close companion of four years, was supposed to have fled, yet here it was still, leering at him with its hideous pale face. He'd been through some of the bloodiest and most brutal battles of the war, yet this was harder than any of them. *Lord, give me strength.*

"I'm truly sorry for your loss," he heard his friend say quietly.

Daniel abruptly took his cup and went to the tent flap where he finished his coffee in one large gulp, welcoming the heat of the liquid. It helped stop the tears from forming in his eyes. If he was going to succumb to grief he wanted to do it in private.

"You need to go home, Daniel."

He had a dozen arguments ready but they died on his lips. While the war still raged further south in parts of North Carolina and Alabama, Lee's surrender had been the beginning of the end. It was only a matter of time now. At any rate, the Army of the Potomac, which the 4th Ohio was a part of, wouldn't see any more action.

His aunt had also sent word that his brothers were dead, but Daniel had already known. He had been at Cold Harbor and seen Toby lining up with a Pennsylvania regiment. He'd been shocked to see him. It had been decided at the beginning of the war that Toby would stay home and help their mother keep up the farm. He'd had every intention of finding the nineteen-year-old after the battle and figuring out a way to get him home. But there had been no chance. His brother died that very day, and having no heart to break the news to their mother, Daniel requested that Toby's commanding officer write to tell her the news. And as for Jonah, one of his older brother's fellow soldiers had written him. His body had never been found, but the man had been positive he had seen Jonah fall in the midst of battle, mortally wounded. With his mother and brothers gone, the farm was his responsibility now. *Like Pa always wanted,* he thought grimly. He turned back to Joshua. "General Grant is most likely still at Mr. McLean's house."

Joshua rose from his chair. "If he's not, we can ride on to headquarters."

Daniel slowly nodded and, putting his cup down, followed his friend out of the tent.

four

Katherine walked down to the edge of the drive and stopped, raising her face to the bright spring sun. With closed eyes she allowed the rays to play and dance on her face before steeling herself to the chore ahead.

She was headed into Ostrander to check on the mail and buy a few things at the mercantile. Mary had written Daniel almost a month ago and there was still no word from him. And with General Lee's surrender a scant two weeks ago, her friend had become terribly worried.

Katherine looked back at the sweet little farmhouse and checked her desire to go back inside. She had to do this because Mary could not undertake the task herself. *Grant me strength, Father.* Making sure her bonnet was straight and readjusting the basket on her arm, she turned and started to make her way down the dirt road.

Her first month in Ostrander had been interesting to say the least, starting with Dorothy Kirby's funeral. It seemed as if the entire township had shown up and crowded into the Kirby parlor. Unfortunately, the viewing hadn't been going on for five minutes when she sensed very clearly she was not a welcome addition to the community. With some there was a tangible, yet polite coldness and they kept their distance. With others it was an occasional barb or remark she was sure to overhear.

Ruth Decker had even pointed out a few people Katherine

should take great care to stay away from. "Oh there's the Hoskins," she would say. "Their son died at the Rebel victory at Bull Run." Or, "There goes Estelle Perry. The Rebs killed her husband at Gettysburg."

But by far the worst comment the woman made concerned a young widow only a few years older than Katherine. Dressed in black, the young woman had seemed so quiet and grave sitting all alone in a corner of the room that Katherine had forgotten herself and made her way over to see if she needed anything.

"Are you quite all right, ma'am?" Katherine asked. She was going to ask if she wanted any coffee, but the words died on her lips at the long stare the young woman gave her. Abruptly, she got up and left the room.

"Adele Stephens." Katherine turned to see Ruth Decker standing beside her and shaking her head sadly. "Such a shame. Her husband was captured and killed when he tried to escape." She grasped Katherine by the arm and drew her closer. "They say it was a South Carolinian who did the filthy deed," she hissed.

"Excuse me, Mrs. Decker," Katherine murmured and rushed outside to see the young widow pull away in a worn-out buggy. She was sure the woman had been crying. Later, she learned Adele Stephens resided in town with her young son, an eight–year-old boy named Jacob.

Now, as she brushed her fingers lightly across her jaw, Katherine could only hope they would not meet today in town. *Father, please bring peace and healing to Mrs. Stephens's heart.*

She was drawing close to Mill Creek Church. As she approached, she looked around. No one seemed to be about, and she quickly slipped through the gate to the graveyard behind the little brick building. She quickly walked through the rows until she came to Dorothy Kirby's grave. Although

Mary hadn't asked her to stop, Katherine had felt she should just to be sure it was neat and tidy. The weather had finally decided it was spring a few weeks ago and everything was blooming. She wanted to make sure a stray weed hadn't sprouted.

Delicate new grass was creeping up the soft mound of dirt in front of the gravestone, and Katherine decided to come back once her task in town was completed. Maybe some spring flowers would brighten her resting place. There might be some blooming closer to the creek.

As she rose, her back protested, reminding her of the hard work she and Mary had been doing to keep up the farm. The work was substantial and constant; Katherine deemed it a miracle they were even able to keep up. Mary had laughed and quoted Ecclesiastes, the verse about how two were better than one.

Katherine had gone to bed exhausted every night the first few weeks. But she was gradually becoming accustomed to her new life. Under Mary's care the blisters that formed on her hands soon healed and formed tough calluses. And she was beginning to wake herself in the early morning rather than Mary calling for her. They would do the daily chores and then set about whatever needed to be done that day. Repairing fences, boiling down maple sap into syrup and sugar, spring cleaning—there was always something to do.

In fact, things had been twice as busy since they had started getting the fields ready for planting. Mary had gone through Dolly's papers when they aired out her room and discovered she had written down what would be planted and where. Katherine had wondered why Mary had been so glad to find the slip of paper until the older woman explained crop rotation to her.

They had started plowing for corn and oats but the day

before yesterday there had been an accident. Mary had tripped and badly sprained her ankle while they were plowing the oat field. She could not put weight on it at all, but somehow Katherine had managed to get Mary back to the house.

Unfortunately they got no more work done that day, a sore blow to their schedule. To make matters worse, Elijah Carr had come calling the next morning while Katherine was doing the chores. They had been forced to leave the plow in the field all night and Mr. Carr had noticed.

"Saw you left your plow out," he'd said as he leaned against a stall door. "Think the field will plow itself?" He chuckled.

Katherine had clenched her jaw and was grateful her hands were busy so he wouldn't notice how they shook. "Mrs. O'Neal took a fall yesterday, Mr. Carr." She filled the horses' feed boxes with grain. "I was tending to her the better part of the afternoon."

"Well, I'll take my team out to your field and finish it off then."

Katherine stopped her work to look at him. "Whatever for?"

Carr's eyebrows raised in surprise. "Who else is going to plow up that field, Miss Wallace? You?"

"Certainly." She quickly walked around him and grabbed a pitchfork. "Your offer is very kind, sir, but I can manage it myself."

The man's face darkened, and it was all Katherine could do to stand her ground until the overbearing man left without another word.

When Katherine finished, she went inside to discover Mary hobbling about the kitchen with the use of a homemade crutch. "I found this upstairs," she explained.

"Mary!" Katherine cried. "You shouldn't even be down here. I was intending to bring breakfast up to you!"

Mary had managed to start the coffee and the bacon on the

black cookstove at the rear of the kitchen. Mornings were still cool enough that they hadn't yet started cooking in the summer kitchen out behind the house. Katherine had been surprised at the need for one. She hadn't realized summers could get so hot this far north.

"Well, I have to admit I'm tired and sore," Mary said as she leaned against the worktable in the middle of the kitchen. "But once I sit a spell, I'll be right as rain. We'll be a little slower plowing today. . . ."

"Oh no, you don't! I declare I never saw the like!" Katherine put her hands on her hips and gave Mary a defiant look. "You are staying right here! I have every intention of finishing up that field myself!"

"Is that what you told Elijah Carr?" Mary asked with a small smile.

"You saw him then?"

"He left here with a look that would spoil milk."

"Before it left the cow," Katherine added. She gently grasped Mary by the arm. "Let me finish breakfast. You go sit at the table in the dining room."

While they ate Mary had mentioned they were drinking the last of the coffee. "I'm sure you won't let me make the trip into town tomorrow." She chuckled and Katherine smiled. It was Friday and they had been going into Ostrander every Saturday if only to check the mail. "We could manage without coffee but"—her face had become etched with concern—"I'm eager to see if Daniel has written yet."

Katherine was so deep in thought, the buildings of Ostrander came into view sooner than she expected. She stopped not far from the Decker house, which was situated behind their store on the southern edge of town.

Ostrander's dislike of her hung darkly over her head. This was the first time she would have to deal with the townsfolk without Mary. Their previous trips into town had been tolerable for Katherine due to her friend's presence; people simply ignored her in favor of speaking to Mary. But what would happen today now that she was by herself? What would happen if she met Elijah Carr?

"But perfect love casteth out fear." Yes, of course. God's love surrounded her and He would surely give her all the strength she needed. And as for everyone else, *"A soft answer turneth away wrath."* Mary always seemed to have a verse ready for any and every occasion, and Katherine had found herself beginning to fall into the same habit.

She smoothed the front of her green floral print dress and adjusted her bonnet. Squaring her shoulders, Katherine walked briskly up to the door of the post office, determined to be as nice as possible to whomever she encountered.

Entering, she saw that May, Ruth Decker's oldest daughter, was behind the counter. The girl was a little younger than Katherine and looked at her with wide eyes.

"Good morning, Miss Decker," Katherine said in her kindest, sweetest voice.

The girl nodded.

"Is there any mail for Mrs. O'Neal this morning?"

May shook her head.

"Well, thank you kindly." Katherine turned away reluctantly. She was almost at the door when a small voice stopped her.

"Are you going anywhere else in town today, Miss Wallace?"

She looked around, surprised that May had actually spoken to her and stared at the girl for a moment or two. "I have some shopping to do at your parents' store," she said finally. "Why?"

The girl bit her lip and wrung her hands. "Folk are out of sorts today. You'd be better off heading home."

Katherine tilted her head and stared at the girl. "Whatever for? What's happened?"

"P—President Lincoln. . . ," May stammered. "They say. . . they say he's dead."

Katherine could feel the blood rush from her face at the young woman's words as she stared at her. *Oh Father, no!* "How? When?"

"I don't know. Pa got the message over the telegraph early this morning."

"Then I must speak with him." Katherine turned to leave.

"Oh Miss Wallace, you shouldn't."

Ignoring May's plea, Katherine left the post office and rounded the corner. She all but flew into Decker's Dry Goods. A crowd of people had gathered, mostly men, but here and there a farmer's wife stood sobbing into a handkerchief. Oblivious to all, she made her way to the counter behind which stood Mr. Decker. "Oh Mr. Decker," she said breathlessly, "what has happened to the president?"

Mr. Decker, a gray-haired man with a long face, gave her a stony look. "Why should you care, Miss Wallace? He wasn't your president."

Katherine stood there for a moment, ready to protest with all her heart until she noticed the dead silence in the room. She turned to see those gathered giving her hard, long stares. Catching sight of Elijah Carr, she felt her knees go weak.

He glared at her. "You'd best be on your way."

"But the president. . ."

"He's not your concern, secesh!" Carr's voice was loud and harsh.

"There's no need to speak to her like that, Elijah," someone said from the rear of the store. "After all, Mrs. O'Neal trusts her."

"And I don't," Carr shot back. "For all we know she knew the man who murdered President Lincoln." He stepped forward and towered over Katherine. "Your pa owned one of those big fancy plantations. You were quite the Southern belle, I hear.

You ever meet John Wilkes Booth?"

Katherine felt the hair stand up on the back of her neck. She swallowed and began to stammer. "I—I. . ."

"Not sayin', eh. Well, maybe you'll be able to tell the county sheriff."

"No," she breathed. "I—I never knew him. I don't want any trouble." She backed away from Carr and her eyes darted around the store.

Near the back she caught sight of Adele Stephens's black dress. The young widow's eyes were red, and she held a white handkerchief in her hand.

Katherine stared at her and tears began to well. "I'm so sorry," she muttered before leaving the store as quickly as she could.

Her tears and the bright sunshine temporarily blinded her, which was why she all but ran over the young man walking down the boardwalk toward the store. She gave a little cry as strong arms grasped her own as they collided.

"Whoa!" he exclaimed in surprise.

Katherine looked up into a pair of soft green eyes, which were intently surveying hers from beneath the broad brim of a Union slouch hat. Dark-blond hair curled slightly at the collar of his jacket, and while she was uncertain of his rank, she had seen enough Union soldiers on her way to Ohio to know he was an officer. In spite of a thin, unkempt beard, he was quite handsome. And quite tall.

A tear escaped and slid down her cheek.

His brow furrowed in concern. "Are you all right, miss?"

Katherine merely nodded in reply. In light of her reception in the mercantile, she had no desire to open her mouth and give away her undesirable origins to—of all people—a Union officer. She could only imagine the look on his face when he discovered she was a Southerner. Looking down, she struggled with the strings of her reticule, searching for her handkerchief.

The young officer released her. "I suppose it is a day for tears."

Catching the sad note in his voice, she looked up quickly, realizing he was referring to President Lincoln. She nodded once more.

He tipped his hat. "May God help us all, North and South," he said gravely.

His comment caught Katherine completely off guard, and she stared after him for a moment as he walked away. He stepped into the mercantile, and she walked out of town surprised to be hearing such a thing from a Union officer.

five

Daniel rode Scioto out of Ostrander with a considerably heavier saddlebag. Coffee, tea, crackers, even some candy—everyone in town was so glad to see him and so sorry over the loss of his mother he was lucky to get away without one of Mr. Henderson's purebred sheep in tow. A small smile touched his lips. *What a sight that would have been.* But the humor he normally would have found in the picture faded quickly. Too much had happened for him to laugh over anything right now.

General Grant had only been too happy to discharge him once Joshua had explained the situation. The great man had shaken his hand, offered his heartfelt condolences, and thanked Daniel for his service. Joshua had helped him pack and ridden with him back to Petersburg where the army had a military train depot. The whole trip back to Ohio had been uneventful, a blessing which gave Daniel time to process the news of his mother's death. He reflected, prayed, and read parts of the battle-worn Bible he had preserved and protected through the war. His mother had been one of the most faithful women he had ever known; that she was alongside her Lord he did not doubt for a moment. But her kind and gentle presence he would miss for a very long time.

Yet just as he was beginning to come to terms with his mother's passing, his world was once again shaken. Upon arriving in Marysville that morning, a town in the adjacent county west of Ostrander, he decided to ride Scioto the last nine or so miles. The horse had ridden most of the way up in freight cars, and Daniel knew his mount would be eager for exercise. He was just tightening the girth on his saddle when a general uproar erupted outside and within the telegraph office. The news quickly ran up and down the streets that President Lincoln had died—killed by an assassin's bullet. Daniel initially found it very hard to get specifics. All of Marysville was in complete turmoil. Eventually he learned of the terrible crime John Wilkes Booth had committed—the single gunshot to the back of the president's head, the wild leap onto the stage at Ford's Theater, and the escape somewhere into the Maryland countryside.

He had ridden to Ostrander in a daze. Daniel had been a great admirer of Abraham Lincoln, and by the end of the trip he still could not believe his president was gone. He had been a good and just man who, like Daniel, abhorred slavery. As Scioto loped along he pulled his leather glove off and flexed the hand the great man had once clasped.

When Lincoln had traveled from Springfield, Illinois, to Washington, DC, on the way to his inauguration in 1861, he made stops in several cities, including one in Columbus, Ohio's state capital. Daniel, then a student at Ohio Wesleyan in Delaware, had made the trek down to see him. Long lines of people stood in the statehouse's grand rotunda waiting to meet the future president. The instant their hands touched, Daniel had been doubly glad he'd been made president. Like his father, Daniel took his first impression of a man from his handshake. The firm, strong grip of Lincoln's hand confirmed all the good things he had heard about the president-elect. No one better could have led the country through the war. And no one better would have led it down the road of peace.

He brought Scioto to a halt. *I don't understand, Lord. What will happen to the country now?* It took Daniel a moment or two to quell the feelings of grief and anger that welled up before he nudged his horse forward.

He looked around him as he rode, and the beauty of his home state surrounded him like one of his mother's quilts. He felt some of his grief and weariness recede. Elm, ash, oak, and maple trees rose like giants on either side of the road. And mixed in with them all, particularly close to the creek, were buckeye trees.

Daniel had carried a buckeye nut in his pocket throughout the war. Some folk thought carrying one was good luck or could ward off whatever ailed the bearer, but he had never held to such silly notions. To him the small brown nut with its large round white splotch was a reminder of home. He pulled it out now and looked at it. In the fall, when the nuts fell from the trees, it had been all-out war as he and his brothers pelted them at each other. But they had always been careful to never bring one near the livestock or the dinner table. While they might be good food for squirrels, the nuts were poisonous to most animals and to people.

Jonah had taken a buckeye with him, also. He had carved his initials in it.

Daniel had laughed at him. "Afraid someone will take it?" He'd chuckled as he watched his brother carving at it with his pocketknife.

Jonah had soberly glanced up at him before returning to his work. "If something bad happens, they'll know it's me."

Grimly, Daniel put his buckeye back in his pocket and looked around some more. The spring sunlight danced down through freshly bloomed leaves, and bright rays of light hit new grass as it poked up through last year's fallen leaves. Squirrels darted and played, running partway up a trunk and, seeing him, dove back into the underbrush. And far back from the road, where the trees grew thicker, Daniel caught sight of a buck with a full rack of white antlers. Even the dust Scioto's hooves were kicking up was wonderfully familiar—

plain brown dirt. No more Virginia red clay, which refused to wash out of his clothes.

At length Mill Creek Church came into view. He stopped out in front and gazed at the little brick building for a moment before dismounting. He tied Scioto to the graveyard fence, and as he looked out over the rows of gravestones, he stared in surprise. Kneeling over his mother's grave was the same young woman he had bumped into in Ostrander. He quietly came up behind her and saw she was arranging some sort of flower on the mound.

"There you are, Mrs. Kirby," she said, leaning back. "Pretty as a picture."

He wasn't sure which surprised him more, her presence or her accent. Who was she and why on earth was this young Southern woman placing flowers on his mother's grave? He was about to ask when she spoke again, still unaware of his presence.

"We still haven't heard anything from your son, ma'am. Mary's so worried. She wrote him almost a month ago." She rose and brushed the dirt from the skirt of her dress. "God willing, Daniel's all right. I'll keep him in my prayers."

Daniel couldn't help but smile at her kindhearted gesture and spoke without thinking. "Thank you."

With a shriek, she whirled around and stood face-to-face with him. Well, almost face-to-face. He hadn't realized how petite she was earlier. Other than that, it was hard to forget such a pretty face. Granted, she wasn't the Southern ideal of beauty with flashing blue eyes and honey-blond hair, but she did remind him of a picture of a simple English maiden in his copy of Bullfinch's *The Age of Chivalry*. There was an appealing sweetness to her face with its pert little nose and soft lips. Auburn hair peeked out from beneath her brown, low-brimmed bonnet and she was staring at him with a large pair of the most incredible eyes he had ever seen. They were a kaleidoscope of green, brown, and amber.

"Daniel?" she asked in surprise. She looked down, her cheeks suddenly red. "Do excuse me, Captain. . . ."

"Major," he gently corrected.

She winced. "*Major* Kirby."

He gave her a long look before suddenly remembering a portion of his aunt's letter he had merely skimmed over, being so preoccupied with the news of his mother's death. She had spoken very highly of a young woman who had come north with her from South Carolina. "Are you Miss Katherine Wallace?"

Her eyes remained wide as she nodded. "How did you know. . . ?

He gave her an apologetic smile as he removed his hat. "My aunt mentioned you in her letter. I'm very sorry I frightened you."

"That's quite all right, Major Kirby. I'm. . .very glad you're home safe. Mary's. . .been so terribly worried."

He frowned and regretted he hadn't at least sent them a telegram before he left. "I'm afraid I received Aunt Mary's letter right as the siege at Petersburg ended. There was very little time to do anything. Then General Lee surrendered. . . ."

"Of course! I. . .I understand perfectly, Major Kirby." Although her voice shook, it was gentle and reassuring. "And I'm sure Mary will as well."

Daniel looked at her curiously. She had to be one of the very few daughters of the Confederacy he had met who had not instantly hated him on sight. A Southern woman's zeal for the cause was almost legendary. He had been spit on, snubbed, and bad-mouthed any number of times. And unlike other young ladies he'd met, Northern or Southern, she made no attempt to flirt with him. In fact, judging by the way she stumbled over her words, she seemed painfully shy.

"I hope—I hope you don't mind, sir," Katherine said, rousing him from his thoughts. "I thought flowers might cheer your mother's resting place."

He stepped forward to look at his mother's grave. "Aunt Mary saw to the headstone," he stated.

"Yes, they put it up just a few days ago."

He saw the flowers Katherine had arranged were a small spray of purple violets, the sort which bloomed near Mill Creek this time of year. He turned back to see she had edged away a little to give him some privacy.

"Thank you for seeing to Ma's grave. Violets were always her favorite."

"There was n—no time"—she quietly stammered, her face flushing red once more—"for me to get to know her well. But she seemed like a very kindly, Christian woman." Her eyes softened. "I'm very sorry for your loss."

Daniel knelt down and ran his fingers over his mother's name carved in the simple granite headstone. Her gentle face filled his mind, and he closed his eyes against the sudden onset of tears. After a few minutes he rose and, as he donned his hat, looked over at Katherine who was dabbing at her eyes with a handkerchief. "Miss Wallace, you mentioned how concerned my aunt is about me, and I would like to get home right away. Would you mind riding with me? My horse is very well behaved."

Her eyes turned to saucers, and she looked at him hesitantly. "Are you sure *you* don't mind?"

He smiled broadly, hoping to set her more at ease. "Of course not." Gently taking her by the elbow, he guided her over to the fence where Scioto stood.

Seeing him, her shyness ebbed a little. She quickly walked through the gate with a smile and stroked his neck. "What a beautiful animal! What's his name?"

"Scioto."

"That's the name of the river Mill Creek flows into, isn't it?"

"Yes, that's right."

"I haven't seen the Scioto yet," she explained. "Mary and I came through Cincinnati and I did see the Ohio River. I must say I agree with President Jefferson. It is the most beautiful river on earth."

He blinked and looked at her with raised eyebrows. "You've read *Notes on the State of Virginia*?"

She blushed twice as hard as before, obviously embarrassed. "I'm afraid I've been looking through your books, Major Kirby. I hoped you wouldn't mind. . . ."

"No, not at all."

This young woman was one surprise after another. She smiled demurely, and as he helped her into the saddle he found himself looking forward to getting to know Katherine Wallace.

six

"How awful for Mrs. Lincoln!"

Katherine patted Mary's hand. They were sitting at the dining room table, she and Daniel on either side of the older woman. It seemed a shame to spoil his homecoming, but they both knew the report of the president's assassination would not wait.

Her friend paled so terribly at the news that she suggested Mary go lie down, but she gently declined and turned toward her nephew. "Who could have done such a thing?"

"John Wilkes Booth," Daniel said quietly.

"I still can't believe it," Mary murmured. "Poor, poor Mrs. Lincoln. How did it happen? Have they captured him?"

"The president was at the theater last night," he replied. "Booth came up behind him. . . . It was a head wound." As Daniel spoke, Katherine blanched and put a hand to her mouth. Mary did likewise.

"Booth's on the run"—his voice turned low and his face darkened—"but the army will get him."

"What will happen now?" Katherine asked. "Will this make the war last even longer?"

Daniel's grave face softened as he looked at her.

"Yes." Mary turned toward her nephew. "Will you be called back into service?"

"No," he replied reassuringly. "I've been discharged from the army." He looked at both of them for a moment before continuing. "I feel the war is as good as over. General Lee started something which cannot be easily stopped. And people in the

47

South look up to him. If he sets the example, many will follow."

Katherine nodded while Mary embraced her nephew. While the news of the president's death had shocked her, she was very glad to have Daniel home. A great deal of worry had lifted from Mary's face when they had walked in earlier, to Katherine's great relief. As they reminisced, she quietly rose and set about emptying the young major's saddlebags.

He was without a doubt the handsomest, kindest man she had ever met. She had been frightfully nervous sitting so close to him on the ride home as she had very little experience with handsome young men. Apart from Thomas, of course. It had been so much easier with him; their relationship had existed chiefly through correspondence. She'd been to numerous balls, of course, but her shy ways and odd coloring meant she had been little more than wall decor, much to her aunt's and father's displeasure.

Words had failed her as she rode home with Daniel. Happily he asked her questions about the farm and Mary, and he was so kind and polite her nervousness eased a little. She told him about what they had been doing over the past month including how Mary had sprained her ankle. But she had not said anything about Elijah Carr's desire to buy the farm. She'd felt that bit of information was best left for Mary to explain.

Katherine glanced over at the young major. She had to admit to being quite surprised that a Union soldier could have such a generous attitude toward Southerners. His voice had been full of respect as he had spoken of General Lee, and he seemed genuinely concerned for the welfare of the South, judging by what he had said to her in town. Even now he was telling Mary the concern he felt over people's desires to punish the South for the war.

She gathered a few things in her arms and carried them to the kitchen. As she set everything down on the worktable, the last thing left in her hand was the coffee Decker's sold. The sight of it was a forceful reminder of the town's attitude toward her. *Daniel is kind but the South got what it deserved.* The thought caused her to bite her lip, hard, and she set down the coffee to finger her scar. She didn't mean that. *It's only right that everyone up here should treat me poorly after how I betrayed Chloe.*

Blinking away the tears pooling in her eyes, she continued her work. After putting everything in its place, she walked back into the dining room to see what else Daniel had brought home.

"I'm so glad you were able to find him," Mary was saying. She looked up at Katherine and gave a sad smile. "Daniel was able to find Toby and give him a proper burial."

Katherine looked at the young major. He was deep in thought and weariness hung heavy in his eyes.

"I couldn't get to Jonah," he said slowly. "He was with the Army of the Cumberland. I was sent word he fell at Kennesaw Mountain in Georgia." He patted Mary's hand. "I'll travel back down to Virginia in a few months and bring Toby back home. Ma would've wanted him buried with her and Pa." He looked out the window for a few minutes before turning back to his aunt, his face grave.

"What is it, Daniel?" Mary asked.

"I got to see Uncle John just before Gettysburg," he said quietly.

Mary's hand went to her throat, and Katherine was sitting beside her in an instant. Her friend's eyes shone very bright as she listened to her nephew.

"He was fine considering he had just gotten over being sick," he whispered. "It was very good to see him."

Katherine felt her own throat go tight, not only for Mary's sake but also at seeing how terribly it affected Daniel. He looked as if he had suddenly aged ten years, his face was so still and grave.

"My friend, Joshua, Uncle John, and I, we ate together a few nights before we followed General Lee into Pennsylvania. Ma had sent me some food." His eyes were nearly beet red as he looked at his aunt. "I found him. . .later. Buried him." He quickly excused himself.

A few moments later, Katherine heard the creak of the pump out behind the house. She swallowed, uncertain of what to say.

Mary simply sat there lost in her own memories, a broken, yet bittersweet look on her face.

"Mary," she whispered.

Her friend looked at her and smiled through her tears. "I'll be fine, dear," she whispered back. "Please, make sure Daniel's all right."

Katherine nodded, rising from her seat. Walking into the kitchen, she could see the young major through the window. He was standing next to the pump in the little brick courtyard situated between the house and the summer kitchen. His hair and face were damp, and he was staring out over the hills and fields beyond the house. She hesitantly opened the simple screen door.

It creaked slightly and he turned around.

"Can I get you anything, Major Kirby?"

He shook his head and turned away, resuming his scrutiny of the farm.

Katherine stepped out onto the porch, uncertain what she should do.

After a moment or two he spoke. "Is my aunt all right?"

"She's fine."

"I shouldn't have told her."

"No!" Her vehemence caused him to turn back to her in surprise. "I mean. . .it was the only news she's ever heard of John. It was terribly hard to get a letter across the lines. She only heard of his death through a friend of a friend." Her voice suddenly caught in her throat. "I only wish you had seen Thomas, too."

He looked at her curiously. "Were you close to my cousin?"

"I. . ." What should she say? That day on the front veranda played out in her mind, and all she could see were Thomas's hurt-filled eyes as she flippantly told him she was no longer interested in socializing with either him or his family. "I cared for him," she whispered, her eyes darting away.

Daniel walked up to her. "I'm sorry."

She looked up. What had it been like for him, all these years, seeing nothing but death and destruction? How many times had he marched men toward their deaths and how many lives had this horrible war forced him to take? He had already buried a brother and an uncle, but had there been others? Four years of combat rested so plainly upon his features that she forgot to be shy and impulsively grasped his hand with both of hers, sensing he needed to feel the warm touch of life.

The look on his face was a mixture of surprise and gratitude as he placed his other hand over hers. He opened his mouth to say something when they heard the sound of a buggy coming up the drive.

They immediately returned to the dining room and found Mary struggling to rise from her seat. Katherine urged her to sit back down as Daniel went to the front window, parting the white curtains for a better look. Having settled her friend back into her chair, she joined the young major at the window.

A black buggy had pulled up in the driveway, and a well-dressed gentleman was climbing out. Her heart sank as she saw who was with him. It was Elijah Carr.

"What on earth is Ma and Pa's lawyer doing here with Elijah Carr?" The young man turned to look at Mary.

"He believes you're willing to sell the farm to him," Mary

said, her voice quiet.

Daniel frowned as a knock came at the front door. He turned to Katherine and gave her a little smile. "Would you please see them into the parlor, Miss Wallace? Tell them I will be with them shortly."

ঞ

As Katherine went to the door, Daniel knelt down in front of his aunt and spoke quietly. "Ma told Mr. Carr I would sell the land to him?"

"Yes," she replied softly.

Daniel sat there for a moment. Since before Ohio had become a state in 1803, the farm had been in the Kirby family. His father had been very determined that his sons follow in his footsteps and farm the land just as his father had. It had disappointed him greatly that Daniel had favored books over sowing a field. Daniel had always resented his father trying to force the farm on him, especially when Jonah, his older brother, had been a born farmer and preferred it over anything else. And Toby had been the same way. Why should it matter if Daniel did not want his share of the farm?

Because Pa saw books as a waste of time, not real work. He couldn't see how a man could make a living reading books all day.

He rose and looked in the direction of the parlor. Ironically, now that Toby and Jonah were gone, their shares of the farm now belonged to him as stipulated in his father's will. And he didn't want any of it. He already had a position to return to at Ohio Wesleyan. His mother had known that. She had always understood his love of learning and his desire to teach.

But to sell the land to Elijah Carr? True, he was a good farmer, but he seemed to think that since his family helped found the county, the entire county should belong to him. He owned most of the land along Mill Creek. Except the Kirby farm.

Pa would roll over in his grave if I sold the farm to him. Of course, he'd roll over in his grave if I sold the farm to anyone.

"He'll give you a good price."

Daniel looked down at Mary. His aunt was of the same opinion of him as his mother. "I know." He gave her shoulder a gentle squeeze before walking out of the room toward the parlor.

Katherine was standing in the hall between the two rooms, her dainty face distressed.

"Are you all right, Miss Wallace?"

She looked up at him. "Yes, Major Kirby, thank you." Before he could ask more, she retreated to the dining room.

Frowning, he continued on into the parlor and was immediately greeted by Elijah Carr.

"I'm real sorry about your ma," he said as he shook Daniel's hand.

"Thank you," Daniel replied stiffly. He looked over at Mr. O'Conner and offered his hand. "It's good to see you again."

The lawyer gave him a small smile as he took Daniel's hand. "Good to see you, too. Your ma was a lovely Christian woman. She'll be missed."

"Thank you. Is your son well?"

"Yes, we missed you helping him with his studies. Too young to join up, of course."

"He was better off. I suppose you heard about Toby?"

"Yes. Very sad. Eliza and I are so sorry for the loss of both your brothers. We—"

Mr. Carr cleared his throat. "I don't believe Mr. O'Conner came clear over from Delaware to talk family."

Daniel glanced at him with slightly narrowed eyes and nodded. "No. I understand you brought him here on business. Why don't we have a seat?"

Once they were settled, Mr. O'Conner spoke. "Daniel, I've been told you're willing to sell Mr. Carr the farm."

"Yes, I've been told the same." Daniel rested his eyes on Carr.

The man looked back at him confidently, not at all bothered by the younger man's statement. He settled back in his seat and smiled.

"I've heard the folks up at that college over in Delaware. . . What's the name?" he asked.

"Ohio Wesleyan," Daniel replied.

"That's the one. Anyway, they're wantin' to make you more than just an instructor now." A grin produced folds of wrinkles on either side of the older man's face. "News of you rescuing a bunch of our boys from the Rebs made its way up here. They're talking about making you a professor."

Daniel thought his heart might leap straight out of his chest, but he quickly reined in his excited emotions. "Well, I'm sure the story was greatly exaggerated. It was only about five men."

"Six as I heard tell it."

"One of the Confederates got Nate Stephens as he tried to make a run for it," Daniel replied quietly. "We tried to go back for him, but the gunfire was too thick."

Carr shook his head sadly. "Shame. His wife couldn't keep up with the farm. I forgave the debt provided she returned the land to me."

Daniel looked away from Carr, irritated. Nathaniel Stephens had not only been one of his men but a good family friend. Their farm had been his and Adele's dream. He had rented the land from Carr several seasons before the war. Jonah had helped him plow up the numerous rocks and build a small frame house. Their son, Jacob, had been born there. Nate had made a good profit even those first years, according to Jonah, so much so Daniel couldn't quite believe he still owed on the property.

Carr spoke, interrupting his thoughts. "Look here, Daniel. You're all set over at the college. If you sell the farm to me,

I'll give you a fair price. With the money you can set you and your aunt up real nice over in Delaware." A look of pure hate crossed his face. "And you can send that little secesh packing back to where she came from."

Daniel's irritation quickly morphed into anger. No wonder the young woman had looked upset as she left the parlor earlier. Whatever issues Elijah Carr had in the past with Southerners, he had no right to take out his rage on such a considerate young woman. He clenched his fist, fighting the desire to strike the greedy, hateful look out of Elijah Carr's eyes. A quick prayer for calm and guidance caused his hands to relax, and the tightness in his chest began to loosen. He looked over at his parents' lawyer. "What's the value of the farm right now, Mr. O'Conner?"

Mr. O'Conner scribbled a figure on a scrap of paper and handed it to Daniel.

He looked at it and knew Carr was right. He could find someplace quite nice in Delaware for himself and his aunt. And while he had no desire to send Miss Wallace "packing," if she had family she would rather be with, he could afford a train ticket for her to just about anywhere.

His heart pounded. He had loved his time at Ohio Wesleyan; his years there as a student and the brief time he had been an instructor at the institution had been very rewarding. He had always dreamed of one day becoming a professor. As much as he admired his family's dedication and hard work on the farm, he knew in his heart farming wasn't his path. In his prayers he had always come away with the feeling becoming a professor was in line with God's will.

This is *Your will, isn't it, Father?*

Daniel nearly gasped out loud at the unmistakable prodding he felt from his Lord.

Looking up, he saw Elijah Carr's eyes now held a glint of

triumph in addition to the hardness and greed which usually rested there.

He rose. "I'm sorry, Mr. Carr," he said quietly. "This farm has been in my family's hands for two generations. I feel obliged to keep it that way."

seven

Katherine opened her eyes. It was still dark but she could hear the sound of the birds' quiet chirpings as they greeted the coming day. She smiled sleepily as she sat up in bed.

The wildlife here was refreshingly different than what she had grown up with—no green anoles scurrying up the walls, no tree frogs making a shocking amount of noise in the evening. And the insects seemed tiny compared with those in South Carolina. She supposed it must have something to do with the weather. It was so much crisper here, not heavy and damp, although Mary had told her summers here could get just as hot and humid. Best of all, her friend had laughingly assured her there were absolutely no gators in Mill Creek. Alligators were a regular danger on the Congaree, and she had never been permitted to go too close to the river.

Mill Creek was therefore an endless source of fascination for her. She especially enjoyed one particular place along its banks where large rocks provided a perfect place to sit and pray or just enjoy God's creation.

As she pulled on an old work dress she had borrowed from Mary, she remembered it was Sunday. The lighthearted feeling she had woken with ebbed a little. She and Mary hadn't planned on going to services today with her ankle so bad. But with the president's death, surely everyone would be attending church. It wouldn't be proper to stay away.

Her mood sobered further as her thoughts turned to Daniel and the aftermath of his conversation with Mr. Carr. She hadn't heard all of it, having been going in and out of the kitchen, but she and Mary had both overheard his refusal to sell the farm. The words had then become rather heated. The young major had kept his temper but Mr. Carr had to be all but forced to leave.

Daniel had gone out to the barn after that, and she and Mary did not see him until supper. He had not said much except to explain to his aunt it would have been downright sinful to sell anything to a man so greedy. After they ate, he gathered a number of things from his room and, after insisting that Katherine continue using it, mumbled something about the barn. She assumed there was a shed of some sort he was making do with, and she felt bad she had chased him from his room. They did not see him for the rest of the evening.

She quickly twisted her hair into a loose chignon. Had he stayed away because she had been so forward earlier? What had she been thinking grabbing on to his hand like that? Daniel Kirby must think her the most brazen woman he had ever met. But the memory of those war-weary green eyes made her wonder what she would have done differently.

She shook herself. *Stop being so silly! He's bound to have left some pretty young thing behind who's been pining away for him,* she thought as she slipped downstairs. If that was the case it was no wonder he had stayed away. He seemed too much of a gentleman to allow a young woman to get her hopes up. *Besides, what would he see in a drab little thing like me?*

Lighting a lantern, she silently hurried out of the house and walked over to the barn. If she was quiet, she should be able to get through the chores without waking him.

The Kirbys' big red barn was nestled into one side of the hill. The upper floor was level with the ground on one side, while on the other, the stone basement, where the horses and cows were kept, was exposed. The upper level stored hay, grain, a wagon, and a four-wheeled carriage. A shed for sheep was built onto the south end of the barn, and the pigs had a separate sty north of the building.

Katherine descended a set of stairs near the hay mow to feed the stock. When she had finished she lingered outside Scioto's stall to admire the animal. He was a beautiful mahogany bay Morgan without any white markings that she could see. And his size matched that of his master's. The horse paused to nudge her shoulder gently with his nose, and she smiled and gently patted his neck as he returned to his feed.

"He likes you."

Katherine gave a small gasp and turned around to see Daniel standing at the bottom of the stairs, a sheepish grin on his face. "I'm sorry. I really shouldn't keep doing that."

She placed her free hand on her chest. "I must admit you do have a way of sneaking up on a body."

"A necessity of war." His smile waned as he spoke and Katherine silently chastised herself. He joined her at Scioto's stall and rubbed the horse's neck. The lamplight fell fully on his face.

"You shaved," she blurted out and immediately felt her face turning four shades of red. She lowered the lantern slightly to dim the view of her face.

His smile returned and he rubbed his face. "I never cared for a beard, especially during planting season. Gets too hot."

"Oh." She swallowed and searched for something to say but he spoke first.

"About yesterday. . . ," he began. He stopped for a moment and Katherine held her breath. He was going to bring up her brazen behavior, she was sure of it. She was shocked when he apologized. "I'm sorry for the way I behaved yesterday after Mr. Carr and Mr. O'Conner left. I hope I didn't upset you and Aunt Mary."

"Oh, th–that's quite all right, Major Kirby," she stammered.

She was relieved when a cow lowed from her pen. "I really should be getting to the milking."

"I'll help. I've been up for a while now. Seen to the sheep and the swine."

"I hope you slept well, Major Kirby," Katherine said as they made their way toward the row of sweet-faced Jersey cows. "I'm terribly sorry you had to sleep in a drafty old shed."

"I wasn't in a shed." A small smile crossed his handsome face. "And actually, it was the best night's sleep I've had in a long while."

"Then where on earth did you sleep?" Her gaze wandered curiously to the spare stall next to Scioto.

He chuckled. "I didn't sleep there either. Come here and I'll show you."

Katherine followed him to the area that separated the horses and cows where a straw mow and the barn's root cellar were situated. He stepped inside the cellar, and she saw that one of the bins had been pushed off to the side to reveal a trap door. Daniel pulled on the door's iron ring and took the lantern from Katherine. He lowered it down the hole far enough for her to see a small room, complete with a cot and a small shelf.

"You cannot mean to tell me you slept down there last night, Major Kirby!" she exclaimed. "All shut up in a hole in the ground?"

He raised the lantern out of the trap door and shut it. "I left the door open while I slept," he reassured her. "I only shut it this morning so no one takes a bad fall."

Katherine's brows knit together. "If I had known this was where you intended to sleep. . ."

"It wouldn't have made a difference." His eyes held a gentle firmness and the light from the lantern highlighted their soft green depths.

She bit her lip and looked back down toward the door, glad

for the dim light. "What is it doing here in the barn?" When he didn't answer right away, she turned to see him looking sober. "I'm so sorry. Perhaps it's none of my business."

"No, it's not a secret. Not anymore." He paused. "My family's farm used to be a stop on the Underground Railroad."

Katherine's eyes widened and her heart began to pound hopefully. "Can I ask... Was there ever a young woman named Chloe here? She escaped during the summer of 1860."

"No." Daniel stepped out of the root cellar and she followed hesitantly, startled at the gruffness in his voice. He stopped by the cow's stalls and after hanging up the lantern picked up one of the milking stools that sat nearby. "By then it was just a hole in the ground." He walked into a stall and sat down. "Time we started the milking."

&

In the silence that followed, Daniel could feel Katherine's discomfort. As she quietly settled down to work in the stall next to his, he regretted being so abrupt. She seemed nervous enough around him already and this surely wouldn't help. After all, she hadn't asked him anything anyone else wouldn't have asked. But his foolish betrayal of a runaway slave when he was ten was still a sore spot for him. *It wasn't her fault my emotions got the better of me back then.*

Within a few minutes the urge to apologize was overwhelming. He was about to speak when her soft voice carried over from the next stall.

"Chloe was one of my father's slaves. She and I were the same age and we grew up together. Her mother was a house servant so she was always nearby. Her father had been sold off not long after she was born. I had never seen slaves as anything other than automatons doing our housework, planting our fields, making us money." She paused briefly. "I had even come to see Chloe that way. Mary taught me they were people, no different than I, with hopes and dreams and feelings and faith. I saw then how horribly wrong slavery was and I so wanted to do something. Your aunt was teaching her slaves to read. Secretly of course. Back then it was against the law. So I began to teach Chloe how to read. Mary told me not to, and I should have listened. When my father found out. . ."

Her voice caught and Daniel rose from his stool and looked over into the next stall.

The young woman sat there small and shrunken, holding a hand to her face, the milking only half-done. The cow twitched her with her tail but she didn't notice. "My father whipped her and sold her off." He could see the tracks her tears had made in the soft light. "I heard she escaped but I never found out anything more." She stopped and, looking away, began to wipe at her face. "Do excuse me, Major Kirby."

He dug into his pocket and handed her his handkerchief. "I was ten. Some boys were teasing me and I blurted out our secret. The man we had in hiding at the time almost didn't get away. Fortunately the law never found the hiding place or else my father would have been fined and possibly hauled off to jail. We couldn't take in any more runaways after that. The risk was too great for them and us."

Her now-dry eyes were filled with compassion as she looked up at him.

"I never found out what happened to him either." He and Pa had asked after the man for months afterward, as discreetly as they could. He hadn't been seen anywhere else in the township, and they had been unable to go ask anyone further north. It had been harvest time and all their attention had been needed at the farm. Daniel had resumed the search himself when he was at Ohio Wesleyan, but the man had never given them his name.

Thoughts of his alma mater gave him an idea. "You said

Chloe escaped in 1860?" he asked Katherine tentatively.

"Yes," she said hopefully. "In June. She was sold to a man in North Carolina."

"Not many slaves from there made it up our way." Since the Appalachian Mountains lay between the Carolinas and Ohio, most runaways from those states generally trekked through Virginia and Maryland into eastern Pennsylvania and up into New England. "A friend of mine from the army might be able to help. I'll write to him and see what I can find out." Joshua Chamberlain knew several people who were active in abolitionist activities, including Harriet Beecher Stowe.

"That's very kind of you, Major Kirby, to go to so much trouble."

Daniel smiled at her continued formality. "I'm no longer in the army," he said. "And before you say it, Mr. Kirby was my pa. I would really rather you called me Daniel."

Her kaleidoscope eyes regarded him shyly. "Then perhaps you should call me Katherine."

eight

Daniel tugged at his uniform as he sat in church with his aunt and Katherine later that morning. He hadn't really wanted to wear the outfit and draw attention to himself, but his Sunday best did not fit him quite right. Poor food and occasional illness during the war had thinned him a bit. Well, home cooking and farmwork would soon cure him.

Thoughts of plowing and planting poked annoyingly at his thoughts, and he returned his attention to Reverend Warren's sermon. The minister was extolling President Lincoln's virtues and exhorting the Body to have faith in these uncertain times. When he quoted Proverbs three, verses five through six, Daniel rolled the verses over and over in his mind. *"Trust in the Lord with all thine heart; and lean not unto thine own understanding. In all thy ways acknowledge him, and he shall direct thy paths."*

His eyes strayed to the wooden cross hanging on the wall behind the pulpit. He couldn't understand the path the Lord was having him take. He had been so sure being a professor was the role he was to play in God's will. And now he was suddenly supposed to farm? Had he missed something? Had his desire to learn and his love for books clouded his judgment? After all, his preference for books had nothing to do with his abilities as a farmer. He was, in fact, a decent farmer. Not as good as his pa or Jonah, but he could easily make a good living at it. Perhaps that fact, Pa's opposition to his schooling, and his now owning the entire farm was God's way of telling him something he hadn't really wanted to hear.

The reverend concluded his lesson, and the Body rose to sing a closing song.

Daniel turned slightly to see if Adele Stephens and her son were still back in the second-to-last pew. They were. Daniel was determined to speak to Adele about Nate and the land she had given back to Elijah Carr. Happily, Carr did not attend church in Ostrander. In fact, as far as Daniel knew, he didn't attend a church at all.

When the song concluded, he turned and saw Adele and Jacob had disappeared. He frowned and started to move out of the pew when he was stopped by Reverend Warren and his wife.

"It's good to see you, Daniel," the older man said as he shook his hand.

"Thank you, sir." Daniel nodded to Mrs. Warren. "Ma'am."

"We're so sorry about your dear mother," the gentle lady said.

"Thank you. Sir, when things are more settled I intend to go back down to Virginia and bring Toby's body back home."

"Of course. We'll have a special service for him."

"It's so good to have you back safe," Mrs. Warren said. "If you'll excuse me." She walked over to Mary, who was already surrounded by several ladies.

Daniel glanced back toward the door.

"Are you looking for someone in particular?" the reverend asked.

"Yes, Adele Stephens. She was here for services, but I don't see her and Jacob now."

"Ah yes, she seems to be slipping out early lately." Daniel noticed the man's gaze rest briefly on Katherine, who was standing quietly off to one side. His eyes turned toward the window. "Why there she is now, climbing into her buggy."

Daniel saw she was just settling into her seat next to her son and, excusing himself, hurried outside. He rushed around the corner to where the young widow was just taking up the reins. "Adele!"

Adele and her son looked back. The young boy smiled and waved at Daniel, but his mother quickly turned around and directed her horse onto the dirt road.

Daniel watched them ride off. He couldn't blame her really. It had to be hard for Adele to see him—the man who had failed to rescue her husband. Being an honest man, Daniel had carefully, yet tactfully, explained Nate's death. He had known Adele; she would have wanted to know. *I should have gone back for him.* But even as the thought crossed his mind, the horrible image of Nate being mowed down by Confederate bullets reminded him he would only have died with his friend, leaving the surviving men to face possible recapture.

Out of the corner of his eye, he caught sight of the shoulder decorations on his coat, which indicated his rank. They had made him a major for saving those men. He'd rather have Nate alive and still been a captain. He turned to find Katherine standing a little ways behind him.

"Do you know Mrs. Stephens well?" she asked.

He walked over to her, trying to read the expression on her face. "Yes, her husband was under my command in the war."

"Oh."

She looked as if she wanted to say more but Ruth Decker came up at that moment. Smiling, she gave him a hug. "Daniel, I'm so glad you're home!"

"Thank you, Mrs. Decker," he replied.

"I saw poor Mary this morning. Said she sprained her ankle. Do you need me or May to come out and help tend to her?"

He looked at her in surprise. "Thank you, but Miss Wallace has been doing a fine job." He glanced over at Katherine whose eyes were lowered.

Ruth glanced at her with pursed lips. "Oh yes," she replied. "I forgot about your guest." She sidled over to Katherine. "I imagine with the war nearly over you'll be leaving us soon.

Won't that be a shame?"

Daniel frowned at the clear note of sarcasm in the woman's voice. He found it hard to believe Ruth Decker had been one of his mother's oldest friends.

He watched Katherine lift her eyes to the woman and calmly answer her. "I'm afraid I have no more family to return to, Mrs. Decker. Mrs. O'Neal assured me I could stay with her as long as I wanted."

"Well, Mary is the picture of hospitality, but I'm sure you must have misunderstood," Ruth said pointedly. "Surely you can't mean to say you have no one you could live with. I mean you can't keep burdening Mary and Daniel. They run a farm, not a hotel."

Katherine looked away with a clenched jaw and reddening cheeks.

Enough was enough. "You're quite right, Mrs. Decker, we are running a farm," Daniel said. "And Miss Wallace has been a great help. She was taking care of things all by herself after Aunt Mary sprained her ankle. I've never seen the farm look better."

"Oh. . .well. . . ," the woman faltered. She turned to see her daughter helping Mary down the church steps. "May, how considerate of you." Giving Katherine a reproving glance, she walked over to them.

Daniel gave Katherine's elbow a squeeze and she looked up at him gratefully. "That was very kind of you," she said. "But I only looked after the farm for a day and a half before you came home."

"And you did a great job." He smiled.

Mary was waiting at the carriage, and as they started to walk over, several people came up and offered their condolences to Daniel. He was gratified by their kind words about his mother and brothers, but he could not help but notice they simply ignored Katherine. One woman even elbowed her out of the way. First Ruth Decker and now this? At first Katherine stood quietly off to the side but eventually walked over to the carriage where Mary was still waiting. It was several more minutes before he was able to join them.

He glanced over at Katherine several times on the way home. She acted as if nothing was wrong, but she was very quiet during lunch and then after helping Mary into the parlor decided to walk down to the creek.

He joined his aunt in the parlor. After several attempts to read a psalm or two, he looked up to find Mary asleep in the high-backed easy chair, her ankle propped up on a settee. He smiled nostalgically. Dorothy Kirby had always insisted on comfortable pieces of furniture in her parlor, and that particular chair had been one of her favorites. In fact, Pa had often woken her as she sat in it on Sunday afternoons. He rose and rescued his aunt's Bible, which had been threatening to fall off her lap.

He wandered over to the window and watched the breeze gently bend the branches of the trees along the creek. His thoughts turned to services that morning, and he shook his head. He could hardly believe the behavior of the people who had been such good examples to him as he grew up. He couldn't recall a time when new people had not been made to feel welcome. When Adele and her brother, Erich, had come to Ostrander, the church people had gone out of their way to help them settle in. They had paid no mind to the newcomers' German accents. But apparently Southern accents were a different issue altogether. He ran a hand through his hair. He was sick of hate and anger. Coming home should have relieved him of that.

The little mantel clock rang the hour. Katherine had been gone for a while now. He frowned. He found he didn't like the idea of her being down by the creek all by herself, especially if she were upset.

In spite of how forward it was, it had been endearing the way she'd held his hand yesterday. And just at the moment he needed to be reminded of life not death.

He looked out the window toward the creek. He had a good idea of where she went—the place where he and his brothers had always gone fishing. Daniel glanced over at Mary, who was still asleep, and quietly left the house, making his way out to the barn. There wasn't much hope of catching anything this time of day, but drowning a few worms was just the excuse he needed to make sure Katherine was all right.

⁊⁊

It had been all Katherine could do to make it home from services and through lunch. As soon as she had helped settle Mary into her chair she made her way across the road to the creek. Pushing her way through the trees, she sank down next to a large mossy rock. Without thinking, she reached for her scar as her chin began to quiver. She had thought by this time at least one or two people would have warmed up to her. But folk were as cold as ever, even more so after what had happened to the president.

Ruth Decker's snide comments echoed loudly in her ears, but her breaking point was Adele Stephens. Katherine had dared a glance back toward her and her son when services had ended. The young widow had such an empty, bitter look on her face that Katherine could not now erase the image from her mind. She leaned over the rock and, burying her head in her arms, wept.

It wasn't supposed to be this way, Father, she prayed. *Is it me? Am I just naturally some sort of pariah?*

How long she sat there sobbing she didn't know. But when a warm hand laid itself on the middle of her back, she was still so upset she didn't resist being scooped up into strong arms and letting her head rest on a broad shoulder.

Several minutes later her tears began to ease, and a handkerchief was thrust into her hand. She looked up to see warm green eyes gazing into her own and shyly took a step back.

Daniel released her, although his hands still rested on both her forearms. "Are you all right?" he asked.

Katherine nodded, not trusting herself to speak.

"You're sure?" She nodded again and he gently urged her down onto the rock he had pulled her up from. "I'm going to try to catch our dinner."

Katherine watched as he took his fishing pole and, baiting the hook with a worm from an old rusty can, cast his line out into the swirling water. The rush of the creek filled her ears and rays of sunshine poked though the green leafy roof, dancing here and there as the wind played through the trees. She took a deep breath. The air had a wholesome, earthy scent. Sitting there taking in the rhythm of God's creation helped her bring her emotions back in order.

Daniel looked over from where he sat at the edge of the creek. "Feeling better?"

"Yes, but you must think I'm the type to cry at the drop of a hat."

He chuckled. "I have to admit I'm beginning to wonder if I should go buy more handkerchiefs."

"I'm sorry."

"Don't apologize. I'm only joking. You don't seem like the weepy type." His face grew serious. "Have people at church been behaving like that since you came here?"

Katherine hesitated. She didn't want to seem like a gossip or a snitch, but neither did she want to lie. Fingering her scar, she looked down.

She heard him give an exasperated sigh. "Katherine, I'm sorry you've been treated so poorly." He paused. "I want you to know this isn't like any of them."

"I know," she replied. "But I can't blame them for feeling the way they do. The war has been hard on everybody."

"That doesn't give them the right to treat you badly. No one should be treated like that by a Body of Christ. It doesn't matter if they're from the North or the South, saved or sinner." He looked out over the creek for a moment before turning toward her once more. "I'm going to take this to Rev. Warren."

Katherine bit her lip. "Mary wanted to do the same thing weeks ago. I persuaded her not to."

"Why?" He frowned.

She looked down at her lap. "Folks already think of me as a spoiled Southern belle. A rebuke won't change their opinions of me. It will only make it worse."

"What they are doing is wrong in God's eyes." She turned to find him standing with his arms crossed and a look of gentle consternation on his face.

He was right. Even if she could talk him out of going to the reverend, she would be letting these people remain in sin.

"Whosoever doeth not righteousness is not of God, neither he that loveth not his brother." The verse rang in her head. *But Father, it will only makes matters worse,* she prayed desperately. But the Lord's call was clear. And in her heart she knew He knew what was best. She looked at Daniel miserably and nodded.

He crouched down in front of her. "Don't look so worried," he said with a small half smile. "Trust God to work it out."

An hour later she, Daniel, Mary, and Rev. Warren were seated in the parlor discussing the situation. Katherine looked at the clergyman warily as he took in all that Daniel had said. He was an older gentleman, slender with round wire-rim glasses and light-brown hair. His generous sideburns were streaked with gray. He looked like a strict headmaster of a boarding school, but Daniel had told her Paul and Minnie Warren were two of the kindest people he knew. She looked away. If that were true she had yet to experience it.

"Daniel, Mary," the man finally said, and Katherine looked at the reverend once more. "You know how greatly your family is respected, not only in the church but in this community."

They both nodded.

"But I have to question your judgment in bringing Miss Wallace here."

Katherine felt her face burn.

Mary pursed her lips.

Daniel's face hardened. "Excuse me, Reverend," he said, his voice surprisingly calm, "but I can't quite believe what I'm hearing. The Word clearly states—"

"I'm not refuting the many scriptures you brought to my attention," he declared with a raised hand. "I just don't think you realize how deeply the war has affected the church and the community." He gave both of them a firm and steady gaze. "The members of Mill Creek Church were very proud to have had so many of its young men go off to fight. But over half of those young men will never return. It has hardened many a heart. And now you're asking them to accept someone who represents the cause of all this."

"You know as well as I do this war was caused by the way the North reacted to things just as much as anything the South did," Daniel retorted. "Need I mention Bleeding Kansas?"

Katherine remembered her father speaking of the bloody battles between antislavery and proslavery settlers as they fought to decide if Kansas would be a free state or a slave state.

"I know that. I only mean for you to understand that it may take a very long time for them to come to accept Miss Wallace, if they do at all."

"If they do at all?" Mary cried. "You can't be serious."

"You haven't been here, Mary. These aren't the same people you and John said good-bye to. Adele Stephens hasn't been the same since Nate passed, and she's been slipping out early ever since Miss Wallace began attending."

Mary, who sat next to Katherine on the sofa, grasped her friend's hand tightly in both of her own. Katherine was too stunned and saddened by the man's words to notice.

Reverend Warren rose.

"So you won't do anything about this?" Daniel's voice was hard as he also stood to face the reverend.

The man's face was strained as he put a hand on the younger man's shoulder. "I never said that. I will address the congregation as gently as the Lord will enable me." He turned to look at Katherine. "Miss Wallace, I can tell you are a sister in Christ and I am sorry if Minnie and I have hurt you in any way." His face grew longer as he continued. "You see, my nephew, Andrew, was wounded in the war, and although his injuries healed, his mind never did. My brother is talking of taking him to an asylum."

"Paul, I'm so sorry," Mary breathed.

"We'll keep him in our prayers, Reverend," Daniel said quietly. "Thank you for coming." He left to walk the clergyman to his horse.

Katherine turned to Mary. "Was the reverend close to his nephew?"

"Andrew was planning on following his uncle into the ministry." Mary's eyes glistened.

Daniel slowly walked into the room and sank down into a chair. "I had no idea."

"Your mother never wrote a word about Andrew or how bad the church's losses were," his aunt murmured.

"You know how Ma was. She hated giving anyone bad

news." Daniel ran a hand through his hair and a heavy silence settled over the room.

Katherine looked at Mary and then Daniel. A thought had been growing on her heart for some time now, and she suspected the idea was not far from their thoughts as well. "I shouldn't have come," she said softly.

They stared at her.

"I'll go back to South Carolina as soon as it can be arranged."

nine

Daniel started at her words and watched his aunt pale.

"No!" Her voice rang out. "I won't have it!"

"Mary, it's for the best." Daniel could tell by Katherine's eyes she wasn't as resolute as she sounded. He tried to catch her gaze but she looked down at her lap. "I know where Aunt Ada is, and if I apologize..."

"No!" Mary repeated and stomped the floor with her good foot. "I won't have you going back to a family whose only value you are to them is who you marry." Her eyes snapped but her voice took on a gentler tone as she continued. "And I won't have you returning to people who would do this to you." His aunt pointed to the scar along Katherine's jawline.

He'd noticed it before but had assumed it was the result of a childhood injury. Jagged and ugly, it looked entirely out of place on her sweet face. A family member had done that to her?

She glanced at him and raised her hand to cover the blemish.

His aunt grasped Katherine's hand and pulled it away from her face. "This is your home now," she said firmly. "I won't hear of you leaving."

"Neither will I," Daniel declared. If that was how her family treated such a sweet-natured girl, there was no way he would let her return to them.

Katherine frowned and looked at Mary. "But what about the church and everyone in town?"

"God can soften even the hardest heart." His aunt smiled. "We'll pray for them. Right now if you like."

At Katherine's nod they joined hands and Daniel led them

in prayer, asking the Lord to bind up the wounds of war and heal people's hearts.

"Thank you, Daniel," Mary said. "It's time we started supper." Grasping her crutch, she rose and made her way toward the kitchen.

Katherine rose to follow her, but Daniel stood and laid a gentle hand on her arm. "How did you get that scar?"

She reached up and laid her fingers against her scar before she answered. "I was trying to protect Chloe from my father's whip. He struck me and his signet ring caught the edge of my jaw."

"I'm sorry. And I'm sorry Rev. Warren's visit wasn't more encouraging."

Katherine bit her lip. "I wasn't entirely surprised. People have been through a lot over the past four years." A shy look passed over her face. "Thank you for praying with me."

"We can pray every evening if you'd like," he offered.

She smiled gently. "I'd like that."

Feeling a little foolish, he watched as she went into the kitchen. In his mind he had hoped the peace that had begun at Appomattox would quickly spread to every heart in the Union. But the wounds of war ran deeper than he had imagined. He hadn't realized how being away for four years had made him so out of touch with those back home.

Bits of Mary and Katherine's conversation floated in from the kitchen.

Real peace needs to begin somewhere. As far as Katherine was concerned, he resolved to be an example to those around him and go out of his way to make sure she always felt welcome in his home.

⁂

A few days later Katherine and Daniel were going about planting the kitchen garden next to the house. Over the past couple of days Daniel had been plowing the fields set aside for corn and oats but, as he had told Katherine and Mary at dinner last night, the newly turned earth needed to dry out before he harrowed. "If nothing else, the kitchen garden can get planted," he'd said, running a frustrated hand through his hair.

Planting was going to be a problem. Katherine and Mary were more than willing to help, but with Mary's foot still on the mend and Katherine so inexperienced he would be lucky to get everything done on time. He would have hired some farmhands, but with so many young men still in the army, help was in short supply. And those few who were available had already been hired out until the fall.

A good many of them had been snatched up by Elijah Carr. *He's still hoping to get the farm one way or another,* Daniel thought as he fetched the gardening tools from the shed connected to the summer kitchen.

His face must have betrayed the anger he felt because Katherine stared at him as they met on the way to the garden. Her kaleidoscope eyes were large with surprise. "Is everything all right?" she asked tentatively.

"I'm sorry. I was thinking about Elijah Carr."

Her dainty face grew thoughtful. "I've often wondered about him." They walked through the garden gate and began a row of carrots. "Has he always been. . . ?"

"Angry, greedy, and hateful?"

"Well. . .yes."

Daniel straightened from covering up the seeds she was dropping and leaned against the hoe. "Elijah Carr's brother and his family moved to the Kansas Territory just when everything was beginning to heat up. He was antislavery and got into a fight with some proslavery men. He was shot to death, and his wife and son were left homeless when the men burned their house down."

"What happened to them?"

"Don't know. Carr doesn't talk about them and no one's ever asked."

A wave of compassion washed over Katherine's face. "That poor, poor man," she breathed. "No wonder. We should keep him in our prayers."

Daniel stared at her. His mother had always told him and his brothers to pray for Carr, to take his pain into consideration and not hold his actions against him. But her words had fallen on deaf ears. Elijah Carr's many attempts over the years to get the farm had hardened their hearts.

Seeing the look on his face, Katherine paused. "I'm sorry," she said. "If you don't want—"

"No, I'm just ashamed of myself," he said softly. "I should have the same compassion for Carr as you do."

"Oh Daniel," Katherine said gently, "he's always been a thorn in your family's side. It's only natural—"

"Exactly. Only natural. We're called to be like Christ. We're not called to give in to our sinful natures. Keep me in your prayers, too. Pray that I can see the man instead of the sin, as you can."

Katherine blushed and quickly returned to dropping seeds in the soft earth.

Over the past week she'd slowly become comfortable around him, but she still never failed to blush furiously whenever he paid her a compliment. From what he'd learned about her family, he imagined compliments had been few and far between. She didn't talk about them very often, but his aunt had told him a great deal.

He shook his head. And he thought *he* had been a black sheep! He watched as she dropped another seed in the ground. From what his aunt had told him she'd learned a lot since coming north. And not just about housekeeping and farming. Since her arrival she had read a number of the books in his collection and had been very happy to talk with him about what she'd read. She'd attended one of the finest schools the South had to offer, but her father had only allowed her enough education to make sure she would make someone a charming wife. Daniel could hardly imagine her being the matron of a plantation, not with her intellect and hatred of slavery. *She deserves a much different life than that,* he thought.

Katherine was now waiting for him at the end of the row, looking out over toward the barnyards where the cows and horses grazed. He joined her, and she turned and shyly smiled at him. Her family may have not appreciated her, but he certainly did. As he looked into her unique eyes he could certainly understand how Thomas had come to care for her.

The sound of a buggy drew their attention to the drive. Mary stepped out the front door as it drew to a halt. A slender older gentleman with a Vandyke beard and wearing a frock suit climbed out. He removed his tall beaver-skin hat and Daniel immediately recognized James Harris, his old professor from Ohio Wesleyan.

"Professor Harris," Daniel said as he walked over. He wiped his hands on his handkerchief before extending his hand, wishing he was a good deal less dusty. "This is a pleasant surprise."

The older man smiled broadly and shook his hand vigorously. "Daniel, it's very good to see you home safe." He peered over Daniel's shoulder to look at Mary and give her a gentle smile. "Mary...," he began and then seemed to remember propriety. "Do excuse me. Mrs. O'Neal, how good to see you."

"James," Mary half scolded, "you've been too close a friend of our family to be formal." She limped over and gave the professor a warm embrace.

Daniel did not fail to notice the slightly reddened cheeks of the old bachelor as they parted. "I heard about both your losses," the professor said. "I'm terribly sorry."

"Thank you," Mary replied quietly. "How is your nephew?"

As they spoke, Daniel turned and found Katherine standing off to the side. He saw the apprehension on her face and smiled reassuringly as he walked her over to his old instructor.

"Professor Harris, may I introduce another good friend of our family, Miss Katherine Wallace? Katherine, this is Professor James Harris."

"How do you do, Professor?" Katherine murmured.

"Miss Wallace, it is very good to meet you," the gentleman said with a tip of his hat. "How nice to hear a Southern accent again. I taught at a Southern university before I came back home to Ohio Wesleyan. What part of the South do you hail from?"

Daniel could not help but smile at the look of surprise on Katherine's face. She'd been so used to people snubbing her as soon as they heard her voice. It was good to see her taken so off guard by his professor's kind comments.

"Why, South Carolina, sir," Katherine said. She paused as a small smile gradually appeared. "On the edge of Lexington County near the Congaree."

"Katherine was our neighbor, James." Mary smiled, grasping her friend by the hand.

"And what a charming neighbor she must have been." The professor's smile faded, however, and he looked at Daniel. "You've heard about the president, of course."

He nodded. "Is there any more news? I won't get to Ostrander until the day after tomorrow."

"Not about Booth, but they have announced there will be a funeral train traveling from Washington, DC to Springfield. Mrs. Lincoln insisted he be laid to rest in Illinois. Our own Governor Brough and John Garrett of the Baltimore and Ohio Railroad were put in charge of organizing the trip." He reached over and laid his hand on Daniel's shoulder. "They say he'll lie in state in several cities along the route they've arranged. Columbus is one of those cities."

Daniel felt his mouth go dry. "When?"

"A week from this Saturday, the twenty-ninth." The professor gave his shoulder a squeeze. "I remembered how you and some other students went down to meet the president when he passed through before his first inauguration. I thought you would want to know."

Daniel looked down. More than anything he wanted to say good-bye to his president but... "I'm very glad you came to tell me, sir," he said, looking up at the professor. "But I can't afford to take even a day away from the planting."

Professor Harris looked at him soberly. "The board got the letter you sent with Mr. O'Conner," he said.

Daniel nodded. His parents' lawyer had been good enough to deliver his letter of resignation to the university after his visit to the farm with Elijah Carr.

"I took the liberty of speaking to him. He said you heard about our offer. I had hoped—"

"I'm sorry, sir. I can't," Daniel replied, looking away.

The professor looked at his former student sadly, and Daniel hoped Dr. Harris wasn't going to try to change his mind. Turning down the university's offer was hard enough. He was relieved when his mentor simply extended his hand.

"It was very good to see you again," the professor said. He then nodded to Katherine and Mary. "Miss Wallace, Mary."

As the professor's buggy rolled down the road, Daniel walked down the drive and across the dirt road. He soon found himself at the bank of Mill Creek. He stood there for several minutes before picking up a large stone and heaving it into the rushing water.

"I don't suppose You're going to tell me why, are You?" he prayed aloud.

He sat down on a low rock near the creek bank and ran

his hands through his hair. The urge to ride over to Elijah Carr's farm and accept the man's offer to buy the farm was so overwhelming he actually stood up.

A professor! They want to make me a professor, Father!

But in spite of his plea, he felt the Spirit close the door on his dream. He quickly walked over to a solid buckeye tree and plowed his fist into the rough bark.

A small gasp caused him to turn around. Katherine stood just inside the shadow of the trees, her eyes wide and a hand to her mouth. She rushed over and looked at his hand.

The skin on his knuckles had broken and blood oozed from the wounds. She looked up at him, her small brow furrowed, and he immediately felt sheepish. He gently pulled his hand from hers and walked over to the creek. Kneeling down, he washed his hand off and sat back down on the rock, avoiding her eyes. He was ashamed that he had lost his temper and that Katherine, of all people, had witnessed it.

She knelt down beside him, her simple work dress billowing out around her, and grasped his hand to take another look at it. "This will need tending to," she said. Her gentle voice didn't hold even a hint of reproach. "We should cover it up in the meantime. Where's your handkerchief? Mine's too small."

Daniel pulled it from his back pocket and looked away. He felt her gentle hands wrap up his wound and felt even more like a heel. "Thank you," he murmured when she was done. She released his hand but he grasped her fingers and squeezed them. "I'm sorry you saw that," he said, finally daring to look at her.

Her face was soft, and an understanding smile graced her face. "It's all right."

He released her hand and looked at the makeshift bandage on his own. "Professor Harris was going to offer me a position as a professor at Ohio Wesleyan."

"I gathered as much."

"You're wondering why I don't just sell out and accept it, aren't you?"

"Mary told me your father was bound and determined you become a farmer. She thinks since your brothers are gone you're keeping the land out of respect for him."

"I would sell this farm in a heartbeat to Carr or anyone else who would give me a fair price for it, but. . ."

"The Lord is telling you otherwise," she finished.

Daniel stared at her, and she blushed and looked out toward the creek.

"You're such a godly man I can only imagine the reason you're doing this is because God is guiding you."

Daniel laughed hollowly. "If I'm such a godly man, why was I about to ride over to Elijah Carr's and accept his offer?"

"You wouldn't have."

He threw a pebble into the creek. "You're right." They sat there for a moment or two watching the creek swirl by.

"If your pa wanted you to be a farmer, then how did you come to be at Ohio Wesleyan?" Katherine asked tentatively.

"Pa died of a heart attack when I was fourteen. After he died, Ma insisted I sell my share of the farm to Jonah and go. She was the one who understood me. Only Jonah wouldn't take it."

"Why?"

"He felt Ma and I were betraying Pa."

Daniel remembered how angry his brother had been. When his first term at Ohio Wesleyan was over he'd stayed in Delaware with Uncle John and Aunt Mary instead of going home. They had owned and run a mercantile there before his uncle inherited the plantation.

"He forgave Ma eventually, but he and I never really reconciled."

He looked over at Katherine to see her beautiful eyes large with sympathy. He found their speckled depths comforting, and he allowed himself to become lost in them for a minute or two. They reminded him of the way the trees looked along the creek in the early fall.

ten

Katherine blushed and looked down at her lap, wondering why he would pay so close attention to her bizarre eyes. She had always thought of them as her worst feature. Her father had always called them "perpetually confused" since they weren't really one color or another.

She could feel Daniel's gaze still on her, and a warm feeling grew in her chest. Why did he give her so much of his attention anyway? He couldn't possibly think her *that* interesting. Could he? She had to admit she enjoyed their evening conversations. They reminded her of the letters she and Thomas had exchanged while she was away at school.

Thomas. She would always miss him, always care for him. But what she had felt for Mary's son was nothing compared to what she was now beginning to feel for her nephew. How could she help it? He was kind, a very godly man. . .*and far too handsome for a drab little nothing like me. He can't possibly think of me as anything more than a friend.*

Glancing up, she saw he was now looking out across the creek. She felt her breath catch as she took in his handsome features.

Closing her eyes she bit her lip. *Oh Father, please take these feelings from me. I know I once dreamed of loving and being loved, but it was never anything more than a dream.*

"Are you all right?"

Katherine started and looked at Daniel. The look of worry in his green eyes caused her heart to pound so hard she was afraid he'd hear it. "I–I'm fine. Why do you ask?"

He reached over and pulled her hand away from her jaw. She hadn't even realized it had strayed there. "Because you only do that when something is bothering you," he said, his fingers curling around hers.

Coherent thought refused to form in her mind and she closed her eyes. "I. . ."

Suddenly harsh shouts came from the direction of the farm, and Katherine and Daniel immediately jumped up and raced toward the house. As they approached, Katherine could hardly believe the scene being played out on the Kirbys' front porch.

Elijah Carr stood towering over Mary, a switch in his hand. She was glaring at the man with young Jacob Stephens standing just behind her.

Katherine gasped as Daniel forced his way between his aunt and Carr, anger hardening his face. "What's going on here?" His voice was surprisingly calm.

"Nothing that concerns you, Kirby," Carr growled. "If you and Mary just step aside, I'll deal with this vandal here myself."

"I didn't do anything," the young boy cried out. "I just wanted to see my home again. Those windows were broken when I got there."

"It ain't your home. That's my legal property."

"No, it's not. You stole it from me and my ma after the Rebs killed Pa."

"You just shut your mouth before I tan your hide."

"Enough!" Daniel hadn't shouted, but his voice was so rough with anger Katherine jumped. With one swift movement, he grabbed the switch out of Carr's hands. Snapping it in half, he tossed it away. "As long as Jacob is on *my* property you won't lay a hand on him."

"He was trespassin' and broke out the windows of that house his pa built," Carr said. "I—"

"Whatever he's done, send me the bill and I'll pay for it."

Daniel glanced back at the boy. "He can pay back what he owes working for me."

"Tore up a couple rows of corn going after him."

Daniel glared at him for a second before going out back to the shed. He returned with a small cloth bag of seed corn which he all but threw at Carr. "I'm sure that will cover your loss. Now get off my property."

Carr walked away from the porch and down the drive, glaring at Katherine as he went.

She ignored him and rushed over to Mary. "Are you all right?"

"I'm just fine," Mary said calmly. "But I'm afraid Jacob got a taste of that switch."

Katherine looked down to see an ugly red welt on the young boy's hand. "Oh you poor thing!" As Mary stepped aside, Katherine knelt down and gently lifted Jacob's hand to look at it. "Please let me tend to this for you."

The boy looked at her in wonder. "Are you really a Johnny Reb?"

"No," Daniel said sternly. "She's the kind young woman who's going to bandage up your hand just as soon as you apologize to her and tell me what happened."

Shamefaced, the young boy looked at Katherine. "Sorry, ma'am." He turned to Daniel defensively. "I just wanted to see our old house. Mr. Carr found me there and chased me because he thought I was throwing rocks at the windows. But I didn't do anything. I just wanted to look. The windows were busted when I got there."

"Why were you trespassing on Mr. Carr's land?"

Jacob shuffled his feet, his brown eyes cast downward. "Sometimes I forget what Pa looked like. When I go back to our old house I remember."

Katherine rose and bit her lip, trying not to choke on the

sudden onset of tears and guilt. Her hand itched to touch her scar but she clasped them together tightly against her waist. *Boys from South Carolina made this child fatherless.* Then another stinging thought crossed her mind. What if it had been someone under her father's command? Or Charles's?

Daniel reached over and rested his hand on the top of the boy's dark mop of hair. "It's all right, Jake. I understand. I know your ma well enough to know she wouldn't raise you to do a thing like that." His voice had lost its stern tone and he looked at Katherine. "I'll go on with the garden while you fix him up. Send him on out when you're done."

Jacob looked up hopefully. "You mean it? I'm going to be working here?"

Daniel raised his eyebrows. "You do understand this isn't going to be easy or fun?"

"I know, Mr. Kirby." Jacob looked at him as seriously as an eight-year-old could look. "There's no school since everybody's planting, and I'm tired of wandering around town. I want to be a farmer like my pa."

Katherine watched a wave of guilt pass over Daniel's face. "You can work here so long as it's all right with your ma."

A huge smile lit up the youngster's face and he looked at Katherine and Mary.

Katherine mustered up a smile. "I believe there might be some peppermint candy somewhere about the house. Isn't that so, Mary?"

"Yes." Her friend smiled. "Why don't we go take a look?"

As she went to follow Mary and the excited young boy went into the house, Daniel grasped Katherine's hand. "I almost forgot about my hand," he explained and then flashed an impish grin. "I like peppermint, too."

"Well, I suppose. As long as you behave." Katherine found herself unable to resist playing along, but she quickly reminded herself friendship was all there could ever be between them. *Handsome men like Daniel Kirby don't fall for women as plain as me.*

&

Daniel was hitching the team up the next morning as he waited for Jacob to arrive. He hoped Adele would let the boy work in spite of Katherine's presence. And his. After all, he had failed to protect the life of her husband, and now he was asking her to trust him with Jacob on a daily basis. Farming wasn't the same as going off to war, but it certainly had its own share of dangers.

Sweat was already beginning to form on his brow. It was going to get warm today. He looked up at the sky in frustration. He was well behind where he should have been at this point in the season.

He shook his head. Jonah wouldn't have gotten behind, even without help. His older brother had been a gifted farmer. He could make every bit of sunlight count for something.

His hand ached as he pulled on a strap, quickly reminding him of Professor Harris's visit. A prayer rose in his mind, but he bit it back. *What's the use?*

Katherine came out of the house just then and walked out to the poultry yard on the other side of the garden. Daniel watched as she stepped into the chicken coop to collect eggs. She'd seemed reserved yesterday evening in the parlor. Even Mary had commented on how quiet she'd been. She'd given the excuse she was tired and left for her room earlier than usual, before they'd had a chance to talk.

He heaved a long sigh. It was going to be a long day today with or without help. He hoped she wouldn't be too tired to talk tonight. Their conversations in the evening were a lifeline, a connection to something now lost to him. *At least He hasn't taken that away,* he thought. *At least not yet.*

He was just about to take the horses out to the fields when Jacob arrived. And he wasn't alone. The boy was walking up the drive alongside a wagon carrying three freemen, one of whom Daniel instantly recognized.

"Simon Peter!" he exclaimed as he strode over to them.

The wagon springs creaked with relief as the man climbed down. He was a sturdy, muscular man, a head or two taller than Daniel.

Unperturbed by the man's height, Daniel looked up at the man with a grin. "Are you still the tallest man in the county?"

"Sure as you're the second tallest," the man joked back and slapped Daniel on the back. "You remember my boys, Aaron and Michael?"

"I sure do," Daniel replied as the two young men climbed out of the wagon to stand next to their pa. Daniel greeted them and glanced in the back of the wagon. A plow, harrow, and other farm equipment lay in the bed. "What's all this?"

"Well, my youngest, Jeremiah, he's been working with them colts of Professor Harris's, training them and all, and he comes home yesterday and tells me the professor says you're trying to work all this land by yourself." The man's normally good-humored face frowned at Daniel. "Now why didn't you come and see me if you were having trouble?"

"Simon, you have your own fields to get done."

"Now, Daniel Aaron Kirby," Simon Peter's firm voice interrupted him. "I done know ya since you was younger than this one here." Simon Peter pointed at Jacob, who was staring up at him with saucerlike eyes. "We got a good start on our planting and Joe and Jeremiah say they can make do. Aaron, Michael, and I are set on helpin' ya plant your crops."

His sons smiled and nodded in agreement.

"And he'd be a fool to refuse your help," Mary said as she shuffled up to them. "Simon Peter, you're a sight for sore eyes." She was lost for a moment as she and Simon embraced. "How's Celia?"

"Miss Mary, it's right good to see you, too. Celia's just fine. Her sister came up a few months back and she's staying with us." He looked past both of them and smiled and nodded. "Hello there, ma'am."

Daniel turned to see a hesitant Katherine slowly approaching. She was clutching the egg basket so tightly he could see the whiteness of her knuckles. He quickly realized how intimidating Simon Peter must seem to someone so small and walked over to her. "It's all right," he said quietly. "This is Simon Peter Johnson. Ma and Pa hid him when Jonah was a baby. He lives just outside of Delaware with his wife, Celia."

"Will I bother him?" she asked tentatively.

Daniel smiled at her tenderhearted nature and shook his head. "Simon Peter has been a freeman for years now, Katherine. I'm sure he'll be happy to meet you. He's a large man but a gentle one." He coaxed her closer.

Mary grabbed her arm and pulled her over to stand in front of Simon Peter. "Simon, this is a dear friend of the family," Mary said, "Miss Katherine Wallace. Katherine was my neighbor down in South Carolina."

"Oh yes. The professor said you had someone staying with you." He bent down and took her tiny hand in his huge one.

"I'm very pleased to meet you, Mr. Johnson," Katherine said softly. Daniel took note of her attempt to blunt her accent.

"Ma'am, folk just call me Simon Peter," he said. "I reckon I won't answer ta nothin' else."

"I do hope I won't make you. . .uncomfortable."

A bright white smile spread across the man's face. "Oh no, ma'am, not a bit. Celia's from down there in the Carolinas. You sound a mite like her." He looked over at Daniel. "We're ready to start when you are."

Daniel looked at the men and, regretting his earlier attitude, silently thanked God for sending him help just when he really needed it. "Aunt Mary's right. I'd be a fool to refuse help now. But I intend to pay you and your sons what's fair."

Simon Peter gave him a hesitant look. "You sure?"

"I won't take no for an answer."

"Well, all right." They smiled and shook hands.

❧

"Wow!"

Katherine jumped at the awestruck voice at her elbow. She looked down to see Jacob still standing next to her. His eyes were glued to Simon Peter who was striding out toward the fields with his sons and Daniel. Katherine couldn't help but giggle. "I know. He's right large, isn't he?"

"He's a giant," the boy squeaked.

"Well, he's a gentle giant," Mary declared, patting Jacob on the back. "What did your ma say about working here?"

"Ma said it was fine for me to work here for as long as Mr. Kirby needed me."

Mary cocked an eyebrow at the young man. "Did she understand why?"

"Yes, ma'am." The boy winced as he reached for his backside. "She understood all right."

Katherine chuckled along with her friend and her heart rose hopefully. She had worried the widow wouldn't allow her son within ten feet of her. Perhaps her prayers were beginning to pay off. She smiled kindly at the boy. "You'd best be off with them, don't you think?"

"Oh yes, ma'am." Jacob ran off and called out to Daniel.

He turned toward the boy and, catching sight of Katherine, smiled.

A sharp thrill rose in her chest and she smiled back.

"Thank you for lifting such a great weight from his

shoulders, Father," Mary prayed aloud.

"Amen," Katherine finished softly, still smiling. Suddenly remembering herself, she shook her head. *Katherine Wallace, if you keep up this foolishness, you'll deserve every bit of what's coming to you.*

She heard Mary chuckle and turned to look at her friend. "Jacob's a funny little thing," she said.

"He is, but that's not what amuses me," the older woman replied as they walked in the house and headed toward the kitchen.

Katherine set the basket of eggs down on the worktable. "What is it then?"

"You and my nephew."

Katherine nearly dropped the eggs she and Mary were transferring from the basket to a large bowl. "What on earth do you mean?"

"You're a fool if you don't see how he looks at you."

"I. . .haven't noticed," she replied evasively.

"Well I have, and he has the same look on his face as Thomas did whenever he got a letter from you."

"Mary," Katherine scolded, "he does nothing of the kind." She continued to stack eggs in the bowl for another moment or two. "Even if he does, why would he?"

She heard her friend give an exasperated sigh. "Father, forgive me, but I would have liked to tell your family a thing or two."

Katherine glanced up to see a pleading look in Mary's eyes.

"Katherine, we've been over this before. When are you going to realize just how pretty you are?"

"When the mirror finally agrees with you," Katherine said gently. Before Mary could get another word in she grabbed the bowl of eggs and took them to the root cellar out next to the house. She set the eggs on one of the many shelves and pulled down several jars of vegetables to take back in for lunch.

Sometimes Mary was too kind for her own good. Pretty is the very last word she would choose to describe herself. *Short, eyes that aren't one color or another, and a head of hair that can't decide if it's red or brown—pretty is the last thing I am,* she thought. Oh, Thomas hadn't seemed to mind her lack of beauty, but then they hadn't actually met face-to-face very often at all. And as far as Daniel was concerned, clearly Mary was only seeing what she wanted to see.

Katherine shut the door to the root cellar and leaned against it as she juggled the jars in her arms. As much as she enjoyed discussing the books she'd been reading with Daniel, it had to stop. If it didn't, she would only end up with a very broken heart. She'd realized it yesterday evening and deliberately gone to bed early.

"Hope deferred maketh the heart sick," she quoted to herself.

eleven

It was easy to keep her resolve that evening. As long as the planting was going on, Simon Peter and his sons were staying at the farm during the week, sleeping in the barn. What had been going on with the Johnsons dominated the conversation in the parlor after supper.

"Are you and your family still attending the church in Africa?" Daniel asked.

The dumbfounded look on Katherine's face made Simon Peter laugh heartily. He then explained how, a year or so before the war, a group of slaves had made their way to Ohio after being freed in North Carolina. They eventually came to Westerville, a virulent antislavery community south of Delaware, and the citizens invited them to stay in some abandoned cabins north of town. They stayed and prospered, prompting one of the few proslavery farmers in the area to label the town "Africa." The new community proudly accepted the name.

Unfortunately for Katherine's plan, Simon Peter and his sons left late Saturday afternoon so they could spend Sunday with their family. Katherine once again managed to get by that evening with the excuse she was tired, but she knew she'd need to come up with something different or Mary would suspect she was getting sick.

However, making up excuses was the furthest from her mind as they went to services Sunday morning. Rev. Warren had promised to speak to the Body this morning. She fought the jitters as Daniel helped her down from the carriage.

"Are you going to be okay?" he asked.

She nodded and tried not to look directly at him. He'd had to wear his uniform again this week, and seeing him in it made it hard to breathe. She grabbed on to Mary's arm.

The older woman found her hand and squeezed it. "Trust Him," she whispered.

They made their way to a pew and sat down. Sadly, nothing seemed very different. Most people greeted Daniel and his aunt but ignored her. She looked around and saw hardened hearts all around her. *Father, please change these hearts by the end of the service.*

May Decker came forward and played the small piano as the reverend led them all in "Just as I Am." At the conclusion of the song, he motioned them to sit and looked soberly out over the congregation of Mill Creek Church.

"It has been only a week since the passing of our dear president. He was a good man and a righteous man. Never was that made more clear to me than when I had the opportunity to read his second inaugural address in the newspaper only a month ago. 'With malice toward none; with charity for all. . .' Those words stood out very clearly in my mind as so noble, so Christlike. He had no ill feeling toward the South, in spite of the war. He said as much just days before he was taken from us. He sought not revenge or punishment, rather, as he so eloquently put it, to 'bind up the nation's wounds.'

"It is time, brothers and sisters, to begin to heal. Even while our wounds are still raw. Who of you when you have gotten cut or burned leaves the wound to itself? What would happen to such a wound? It would become angry and fetid and you would suffer the effects of such an infection. It is the same now with our country, our community, and our church. We must bind up the wounds left in our hearts and allow them to heal.

"'Whosoever doeth not righteousness is not of God, neither

he that loveth not his brother.' President Lincoln clearly understood and accepted that verse. He was a true believer. If we are to be true believers, if we are to honor the memory of our president, we must love our brothers and our sisters in Christ. Be they Northern or Southern.

" 'There is neither Jew nor Greek, there is neither bond nor free, there is neither male nor female: for ye are all one in Christ Jesus.' Let us treat one another without malice and let us love one another as Christ has called us."

⁂

It hadn't been a long sermon but it had made its point. At least Daniel prayed it would. He watched as the preacher stepped away from the simple wooden lectern and reached out to shake Katherine's hand.

She took his hand readily in her own and gave the reverend a gentle smile.

Giving her a somewhat sad smile in return, the man turned and nodded to May who began a new hymn, the one usually played before communion was served.

Daniel was gratified at first by the people who came up to them after services to greet Katherine. But it was tempered by their cold manner and how few made the effort.

Frustrated, he stepped outside and walked over to the carriage.

"I did warn you, Daniel." He turned to see the reverend standing behind him.

"I had hoped for more," Daniel replied. "I would have thought your example. . ."

"It will take more than my example to change people's hearts. They need time and prayer."

Daniel sighed and changed the subject. "I didn't see Mrs. Warren this morning."

Rev. Warren looked away. "She didn't feel up to coming

today."

Daniel was about to reply when he saw Katherine and Mary walking out the church door accompanied by May Decker. The younger girl was speaking very animatedly to Katherine, whose face was lit up by a broad smile.

He turned to the clergyman with a grin. "Maybe there's reason to hope after all."

"He's supposed to be returning home soon," May was saying as they approached.

"I'm so very glad for you," Katherine replied.

At that moment William and Ruth Decker quickly walked up to them. Mr. Decker looked at his daughter sternly. "May, go wait by the wagon."

"But Pa..."

"Do as your pa says, young lady," Ruth commanded. When May had gone, she turned on the reverend. "Rev. Warren, I must say this may be the last time we grace the walls of this church with our presence."

"Ruth!" Mary gasped.

"As much as this body of believers has been through, I'm surprised at you," she plowed on. "Why, poor Adele Stephens didn't even come this morning."

Daniel walked over to stand beside Katherine as she lowered her eyes. "Yes, Mrs. Decker, I noticed. But as I said—"

"Might I remind you of the punishment the good Lord meted out to Sodom and Gomorrah? The South deserves no less for all it's put us through."

"Those were unrepentant cities, Mrs. Decker," Daniel said evenly. "Miss Wallace is a sister in Christ."

"And she's always been loyal to the Union," Mary added.

"Be that as it may, the fact remains she makes more than one person uncomfortable," Ruth declared. "Why, people have a right to worship in peace."

Several other people standing nearby nodded.

"As you can see, we are not the only ones who feel this way. Perhaps it would be best if Miss Wallace stopped attending Mill Creek Church."

"Ruth, she'll do nothing of the sort," Mary retorted.

"Of course not," Daniel added.

"I'll do it," Katherine said softly. Daniel stared at her and she returned his gaze with firm eyes. "I don't want to be any trouble."

&

Later that afternoon, Daniel was out back in the courtyard setting up his mother's quilting frame.

Both he and Mary had begged Katherine to reconsider her decision to not return to church, but her mind was made up. She said she would sit in the parlor and read her Bible while they were at services. "I'll be able to keep a close eye on lunch," she declared. "Even have it ready and waiting when you both get home. There's nothing like a warm meal after services."

Daniel took one of the chairs he had brought from the porch and set it near the frame. Leaving it, he walked over to the garden fence and leaned against it, looking out over the poultry yard and the fields and trees beyond.

Why, Lord? he prayed. *I don't understand any of this. You want me to farm instead of teach, and now this business with the church and Katherine. . . Why didn't You soften their hearts?* He knew the words were hard, but his ma had taught him to pray without holding anything back. "He knows what you're feeling anyway," she had once said. "So long as it's respectful, you might as well speak your mind."

He heard the screen door creak, and he turned to see Katherine walking out with a quilt top neatly folded across her arm. Mary had found it among his mother's things. Most of the blocks had already been pieced together, and it hadn't taken his aunt long to finish getting it ready for quilting. They realized it must have been meant for Jonah based on the simple design and the fact Dorothy had mentioned it in her last letter to Daniel.

Katherine smoothed her hand over it, admiring the workmanship. "This is pieced so beautifully. Your mother was a good sewer." Seeing the look on Daniel's face, her smile faded. "It's all right Daniel, really. Rev. Warren said it would take time." She laid the quilt top over the back of the chair and joined him at the fence.

"They've known you for a month and a half now. How much more time do they need?"

"We have to give them time," she said, raising her eyes to his. "You told me to trust God to work it out."

"And you can't be present at services for Him to do that?"

"No. It would be best if I stayed away. For now anyhow." She looked down at her hands, which were clasped tightly together as she leaned them on the fence. He knew immediately she was struggling not to touch her scar.

"Are you doing this because you feel it's the right thing to do or because you feel you deserve it?"

"Daniel, the war has been hard on everyone. What the South did—"

"Has nothing to do with you." He took her by the arms and turned her to face him. "You are not responsible for the war. Or their heartache."

She looked down. "I'm responsible for what happened to Chloe. My family owned slaves. And my brother and father fought for the South."

"That has nothing to do with it."

"But what if I *am* responsible for what happened to Adele Stephens?"

Daniel stared at her. "What do you mean?"

"Adele's husband was killed by a Confederate soldier from South Carolina. My father was a general and my brother a lieutenant colonel. What if it was a man under my father's command? Or my brother's?"

Daniel closed his eyes and took a deep breath. "Nate Stephens was one of six men who were captured by a small group of Confederates. They were all men under my command and they had accidently crossed the lines during the confusion of battle. I managed to sneak in and free them. Nate had a leg wound and had fallen behind when Confederates realized they were gone. When I turned to look for him, they fired."

"Who—?"

"I don't know where they were from. No one did. And no one probably ever will." He let go of her and let his hands drop helplessly at his side. "If anyone is responsible for his death it's me."

"Oh Daniel, I'm so sorry. Ruth Decker said—" She stopped and bit her lip. "I should have known better."

"It's not your fault."

"It's not yours either."

"I should have gone back for him."

"No. Then you both would have died."

The look of horror in her eyes told him just how deeply she cared for him and the sweet realization struck him like a cannonball. Her eyes softened as he looked at her, and he slowly reached up and brushed a stray hair away from her cheek. An almost panicked look crossed her face and she quickly walked back over to where she had laid the quilt top.

If she was worried whether or not he cared for her she had no reason to be. Daniel just then realized he'd loved her since the first moment he'd looked into her kaleidoscope eyes.

twelve

Katherine was so dizzy she was obliged to pick up the quilt top from the back of the chair and sit down. Daniel was still looking at her, and she made a show of examining the fabric in her lap as if looking for loose strings. Had she revealed too much in answering him the way she did? She could hardly help herself. The thought of his lying dead on some Southern battlefield had torn at her heart. Why had he touched her like that?

He's grateful for what you said, that's all, she firmly told herself. *Someone like him would never—could never—think about you.*

She heard him walk over and continue to put together the quilt frame. Frantically, she searched her mind for something to say. "This is stitched so beautifully. Mrs. Kirby was a wonderful sewer," she said and immediately winced, realizing she had already said as much.

She was relieved he didn't seem to take note of that fact as he slid the long poles through the holes in the I-shaped legs. "Thank you. Ma was one of the best quilters in the township. I remember Pa setting this up for her out here, and ladies from miles away would come and quilt with her." He grabbed the other dining room chair and set it close to hers and straddled it. "Did Aunt Mary show you the quilt my grandmother made for Ma when she married Pa?"

Her eyes brightened. "Oh yes, it was lovely." She ran her hand over the frame. "Did this belong to your grandmother?"

"Pa made this for Ma when they got married. Every quilt in the house was made on this frame."

"I found some lovely pieces of fabric in your mother's rag

bag." She gave him a sympathetic look. "Mary told me she was saving them for your sister."

Daniel nodded. "Ma lost more than one baby between me and Jonah. She had Rebecca Ann before Toby. She died before she was even a month old."

"I'm so sorry. Do you remember her well?"

Daniel shook his head thoughtfully. "No. I was only three. I remember Ma being sad, though."

"I'll leave them be, then."

"Why? Were you going to do something with them?"

"I was thinking of making a quilt with them." She waved her hand. "I don't have to."

"No, go ahead. Ma would have loved the idea of making something beautiful with her fabric." His green eyes found hers. "I know she would have loved you, as well."

Katherine paused before answering, trying to get her pounding heart under control. "I wish I could have known her better."

"Actually you do," he replied thoughtfully. "She was a lot like Aunt Mary." He leaned forward against the back of the chair. "Just how did you meet Aunt Mary and Uncle John? We've talked quite a bit but never about that."

"No, we haven't." She looked toward the house, wishing Mary would come out. She had shooed Katherine out of the house, insisting on cleaning up the lunch dishes herself as her ankle was doing much better. But Katherine knew her friend's true motive. *Doesn't she see I haven't a chance with him?*

Realizing she couldn't avoid *all* conversation with him, she proceeded to tell Daniel about how she had met Mary and how they had corresponded while she was at school. "She became sort of a mother to me," she said softly.

"What about your aunt?"

"Oh, she was of the same opinion as my father. 'Get the drab little thing married off as quick as we can,' she'd say."

"Drab little thing? That hardly describes you."

Katherine flushed at the glint in Daniel's eyes. "Anyway, John and Mary were very good to me."

"And Thomas?"

Katherine noticed the slight tension in his voice. "We exchanged letters as well. But nothing ever happened between us."

"You told me you cared for him."

"I did. But. . ." She looked away miserably. "I managed to ruin any chance I had with him. After everything that happened with Chloe, my father made me personally break off our acquaintance. I'm afraid I was quite flippant with him." She'd had to be. Or face her father's whip.

She felt Daniel take her hand, and of their own volition, her eyes found his.

He looked at her intently. "Katherine, stop taking the blame for things completely out of your control." His eyes made her feel faint. "If I knew my cousin, he understood."

❧

On Tuesday morning, Katherine looked out the kitchen window for the hundredth time.

Mary looked up from the ironing. "Is he coming yet?"

"No, not yet."

Jacob had not shown up at the farm yesterday morning, and when he hadn't come again this morning, Daniel had decided to take the wagon and find out what was going on. It was almost lunch and he still hadn't returned.

Katherine turned from the window to look at Mary. "It's me, isn't it?"

The older woman gave her a look of reproach. "No. Don't think that."

"I can't help but think about why she wasn't at services on Sunday."

"She could have been under the weather."

As Katherine returned to sprinkling items for Mary to iron, she couldn't help but feel a sense of loss about the whole situation with Mill Creek Church. In spite of how people had treated her she had enjoyed worshipping there. The songs they sang were rich and faithful and sung with such feeling. And in spite of her initial misgivings, Rev. Warren was a gifted preacher. So it had been hard for her to stand her ground when both Daniel and Mary had tried to convince her to go with them Sunday. But she had promised and didn't want to cause trouble.

In fact, she was still toying with the idea of leaving altogether. It would be easier for them to move on as the reverend had asked them, wouldn't it?

Lord, I felt Your hand in my decision to come here, but now, more than ever, I can't understand why. It makes much more sense to leave these people in peace.

Dipping her hand into a bowl of water, she sprinkled one of Daniel's shirts—the white one he wore with his uniform. Her heart pounded and her hands shook as that dashing image of him rose in her mind.

She clenched her teeth in frustration. *Please, Father, I need to leave before I lose my heart even more to this man,* she begged. She sighed at the answer in her heart. There was nothing else to do but trust Him. Even if it meant having her heart broken.

As she rolled up the shirt she began to form a new, yet truthful excuse that would allow her to go to bed early that night. Happily, Simon Peter and his sons would be here. If Daniel got to talking to them first, he wouldn't notice if she slipped out early.

Mary laid her iron back on the hot cookstove and carefully folded the dress she'd been working on. "We'd best clear up in here and get lunch started," she said with a sigh. "Simon Peter and the boys will be in soon."

Katherine began to gather up the rest of the clothes when

she caught movement out of the corner of her eye. She looked through the window to see Scioto tearing down the road with the wagon, Daniel leaning forward in the seat urging him on. As they swept by, her heart nearly stopped at what she thought were two bodies lying in the bed of the wagon, but it went by too fast for her to be sure.

By the time she and Mary made it to the front door, Daniel was out of the wagon, yelling for them and Simon Peter.

Katherine raced to the wagon as Daniel lowered the bed door. "Oh no!" she gasped. Adele and Jacob lay in the bed on quilts, pale and still.

Daniel climbed in and laid a hand on the young boy's forehead before swinging him up into his arms. He looked around wildly. "Where's Simon Peter?"

Before she could answer, he was there. One look and he took the boy from Daniel. Jacob looked like a rag doll in the large man's arms. Aaron and Michael ran up, and Aaron, who was built more like his father, took Adele. Katherine heard Mary tell them where to take them, but her eyes were fastened on Daniel, who watched them being taken inside.

"This is my fault," he said raggedly.

"How could it. . . ?"

"If Nate had been here none of this would have happened."

"Daniel, you don't know that."

"Go see what you can do. God have mercy on me if something should happen to them." He sank down against the wagon's side wall and put his head in his hands.

Katherine picked up her skirts and raced into the house and up the stairs.

The door to Jonah's room was shut, and Simon Peter and his sons filled the small hallway. She could see by the looks on their faces they wanted to be doing something other than just standing around.

"Can you go see to Daniel?" she asked softly. "I'm afraid he's in quite a state."

Simon Peter nodded, and he and the boys immediately walked downstairs.

Opening the door to Jonah's room, she walked in to find Toby's old trundle bed had been pulled out. Mary knelt next to it tending to Jacob while Adele lay quiet and still on Jonah's bed. Katherine gasped at the sight of the boy's hand, the same one she had bandaged up only a few days ago. It was quite swollen and a violent shade of red. Worse still, the swelling was beginning to spread to his wrist.

Mary looked up. "Katherine, before you even think it, it's not your fault," she stated firmly. "He's been helping with the planting for the past couple of days. Boys being boys, it's had plenty of chances to get infected."

Katherine looked over at Adele and started. "Mary, she looks half-starved!"

"I know," the older woman replied grimly. "I loosened her stays, but there's barely anything there to cinch in."

Katherine sank down on the edge of the bed and placed a hand on Adele's forehead. "She hasn't any fever."

"No, but Jacob's burning up." The older woman rose. "Stay with them." She left, and Katherine knew she was headed for the section of the pantry that held Dorothy Kirby's collection of dried flowers and herbs.

When Mary sprained her ankle, she had instructed Katherine on how to use them to treat her injury. "My mother," she'd said, "learned a thing or two from the Indians before they were forced to move west. She passed on what she knew to Dolly and me."

But as Katherine now looked helplessly at Jacob's swollen hand and flushed face she wondered how a few shriveled leaves could possibly help now. A prayer formed in her mind and she closed her eyes. They opened the very next instant, however, as she heard Adele mutter and stir.

"*Mein lieber, Junge!* Jacob!" Her eyes opened and she looked around blearily. "Where is he?"

"Shh, Mrs. Stephens," Katherine said softly. She hoped the woman was too delirious to know who she was. "He's here. Mary's going to take right good care of him."

To her relief Adele seemed to calm down and slipped back into unconsciousness.

Katherine resumed her prayer and did not cease until Mary returned with a steaming mug.

"I have Daniel digging up one of Dolly's coneflowers," she said. "The roots she had were too old to use. Come here and help me sit him up."

"What's that?"

"This is tea brewed from dogwood bark. The Delaware Indians use this to control fever."

They sat Jacob up and managed to get a few sips down his throat.

"There," Mary said once they had settled the shivering boy back beneath the quilt. "I'll use the coneflower root to make a poultice. It'll help draw out the infection." She placed her hand on Katherine's and smiled. "And you've already been about the most important step, prayer."

"What about Adele?"

Mary pursed her lips slightly. "Prayer as well, along with a little food and a generous dose of common sense."

The sound of boot steps downstairs in the hall told them Daniel had finished his task. They went down and found him sitting in the parlor.

Mary nudged Katherine in his direction while she went to the kitchen.

He stood up as she stepped in the room. "Aunt Mary said it

isn't as bad as it looks."

"She told me the root you dug up will help."

He nodded. "Ma used coneflower a lot." He ran a hand through his hair. The guilty look from earlier began to creep back into his face.

"This isn't your fault, Daniel," Katherine said firmly.

"Nate should be here," he snapped. "And so should Jonah. And Toby. And Ma." Katherine watched as he began to pace the room. "Why should I keep going on like this? I have what I've always wanted waiting for me at Ohio Wesleyan. Give me one good reason why I shouldn't sell out and be done with it?"

" 'Trust in the Lord with all thine heart,' " she quoted tremulously, " 'and lean not unto thine own understanding.' "

Daniel stopped his pacing and stared at her before walking over and pulling her into his arms. He buried his head in her small shoulder, and she found herself standing on tiptoe to return the embrace. Her fingers brushed his silky hair and she marveled at how right it felt to be in his arms.

Don't fool yourself. He's hurting right now. Nothing more.

After a moment or two, he lifted his head but didn't release her. Instead he looked deeply into her eyes. "Did you finish that book of Wordsworth's poems?"

She nodded, too worked up over the way he was looking at her to speak.

"Discuss it with me tonight. Don't run off so soon after dinner." He must have read the hesitancy in her face for he pressed her further. "Please. If I can't teach at least there's that."

She nodded and stepped away from him. "I better see if Mary needs me."

She turned and headed toward the kitchen, a hand over her wildly pounding heart. A part of her was beginning to believe what she had thought to be quite impossible.

thirteen

Mary and Katherine took turns seeing to Adele and her son. By the next morning Adele was awake and lucid, and Katherine told Mary it might be best if she helped her with the simple broth they had been feeding her. *The poor woman has enough to deal with. She doesn't need the likes of me around,* she thought as she settled down with the mending in the dining room.

She was surprised when Mary came back down the stairs a moment or two after going up to see to the young widow.

"What is it? Is it Jacob?" she asked.

Mary shook her head. "No, but I need to make up a new poultice for him." She laid a gentle hand on Katherine's cheek. "Adele wants to see you."

Katherine's eyes widened, and she looked at the stairs and then back to her friend.

Mary patted her shoulder. "Go on up. She's waiting."

Leaden weights seemed to replace Katherine's feet as she walked up the stairs. She reached the door of Jonah's room and peered in.

Adele was propped up in bed, her thin hands holding the mug of broth Mary had brought her. It sat in her lap half lost in the folds of the light quilt covering her. She was staring down at her son, who lay in the little trundle bed next to her. They had managed to bring his fever down a little, but his hand was still red and swollen.

Tears pricked at Katherine's eyes as she saw the worried look on Adele's face. She slowly walked into the room, and the young widow immediately turned her head toward her.

Katherine attempted a weak smile as she sank down in the chair next to her bed. "Good morning, Mrs. Stephens," she said and inwardly winced at the sound of her own voice and how much it must distress the poor woman.

"My son, how is he?" she asked, her weak voice revealing her German heritage.

"His fever is down a little. Mary is making up a new poultice." She wondered why Adele had called her up merely to ask what Mary could very well have answered.

"I tried all I knew. But he became so sick." She lifted the mug she held to her lips, but her hands shook and Katherine immediately steadied it as she took a sip. She let Katherine take it from her and leaned back against the pillows. "How did we get here?"

"Daniel came looking for you when Jacob didn't show up." Daniel had told them the evening before how he had pounded on the door to their small shack at the edge of town. When there was no answer he peered in a window and broke in when he had seen Adele lying in a heap on the floor. "He brought you both here."

"The infection set in so quickly," she said tearfully.

"Why didn't you send for the doctor?"

"I could not afford it." Adele looked brokenly at her son. "Mein lieber, Junge. God is punishing me."

Katherine stared wonderingly at her. "I'm afraid I don't understand, Mrs. Stephens."

Adele reached out a weak hand and laid it on Katherine's. "*Weil ich tadelte*—" She stopped herself. "Because I blamed you for Nathaniel's death," she continued softly, her accent becoming thicker as her emotion rose. "Mrs. Kirby was helping me after I lose the farm. But when you come I cannot bring myself to talk to Mary." Katherine's free hand strayed to her jaw as the poor woman continued. "We were running out of food. It is why I let Jacob come here. So he could eat. You were so kind to him he says. He says I should not be angry." She dissolved into tears.

Katherine shakily offered her a handkerchief before calling for Mary. The older woman arrived and Katherine left the room, unable to hold back tears of her own.

❧

By that evening Adele was well enough to be helped downstairs into the parlor. Since her confession to Katherine earlier she kept to herself, communicating with them through nods and short one-or-two-word sentences. Jacob, while he showed some improvement, was still very sick.

Mary insisted Adele leave his side for at least an hour or so. She promised to stay with him while Katherine made dinner.

When Daniel stepped into the house, he found Adele seated on the sofa, one of his mother's quilts lying over her lap. He immediately started to leave the room.

"Daniel," she called.

He slowly stepped back in. Still weak and thin, Adele looked nothing like the woman Nate had left behind. Her blue eyes were dull and her corn silk-colored hair was thin and dry. He still couldn't believe how wasted she'd become. But she looked at him kindly and asked him to sit down next to her.

"Adele. . . ," he began and then stopped. The words he'd rehearsed over and over in his head refused to come to him. He could only look at her helplessly.

"It is good to see you again." She looked at him for a moment or two and sighed. "I am sorry. I should have written to you."

"No," he said slowly. "I never should have told you what happened the way I did."

"No, it needed to be told." She patted his hand. "I will be able to tell Jacob how brave his father was when he is older." Her face became even more drawn. "If my pride has not killed him."

"Adele, what happened?" he asked eagerly. "How did you get so sick? Why did Elijah Carr make you leave your farm?"

"I could not take care of the land. When Nathaniel died I had to let go of the help and I could not keep up. So I gave it back to Mr. Carr."

"He said something about a debt. I thought Nate had the land paid off."

She lowered her eyes. "I borrowed money from him. So we could eat. He forgave the debt when I gave him back the land."

Daniel frowned. "Ma should have told me."

"I would not let her."

"What about your brother? Why didn't you write him?"

Adele looked at him sadly. "I tried to write him but he never wrote back."

Daniel ran his hands through his hair. Erich had gone west not long after Adele had gotten married. He'd always written religiously. Therefore, the only explanation was that he had perished somewhere in the Western plains like so many others. "Ma should have told me. I could have sent or done something."

"Your mother did it for you," she reassured him. "She got Mr. Henderson to let us live in his old building in Ostrander. And she would bring us baskets of food." Her own brow furrowed. "But then she got sick. I did not even know until Mr. Carr brought the last basket. He said I should stay away so we would not get sick, too." She closed her eyes and raised a hand to her face. "I came here for your mother's funeral, to speak to Mrs. O'Neal. But Miss Wallace spoke to me first and I left. I could not come back." Adele bowed her head, shamefaced. "I did not want to see her again."

Daniel started. His mother had died almost two months ago. "Adele, how long have you been without food?"

"I stretched out what I had left from the last basket," she

whispered, still looking down at her lap. "I let Jacob have most of it. But it ran out. I was too proud to say anything to those at church. So I had to come let him work for you even though I did not want him with Miss Wallace. He needed to eat." Tears welled up in her eyes. "She was so kind to my son. She bandaged his hand and gave him candy. I had treated her so poorly. Jacob said I needed to forgive. I was going to come to church last Sunday to apologize. But he got sick and I don't remember what happened after that."

Daniel scooped her up in his arms and let her weep into his shoulder as he closed his eyes and silently worded a prayer.

ꝫ

Two nights later Daniel sat in the parlor as Katherine worked on some mending. He watched her delicate hands work needle and thread to repair the breast pocket of one of his work shirts. When she finished, she smoothed her hand over the pocket before setting it aside. He'd never wanted to be a piece of fabric so much in his life.

Daniel shifted in his seat and tried to focus his gaze on something else, the wall, the clock, anything other than the lovely creature who sat so near him but still seemed beyond his reach. He'd wanted to talk to her since that day at the fence. He had been certain she felt something for him, too. Had he imagined what he had seen in her eyes?

They'd had such an enjoyable discussion two nights before, and she seemed happy as they had laughed and talked. But now she was suddenly distant again. If it wasn't for Simon Peter sitting at the secretary reading the *Delaware Gazette* and Aaron and Michael playing checkers on the floor, he'd kneel down in front of her and beg her to talk to him.

He glanced at the mantel clock. Mary was upstairs with Adele and Jacob, and if Simon Peter and his sons went out to the barn when they usually did he might be able to speak with her before she went upstairs. Leaning back on the sofa, he opened up the book he and Katherine had been discussing. He read the first line of "Lines Composed a Few Miles above Tintern Abbey. . ." at least a dozen times before Michael finally yawned.

"It's early yet, but I'm done in." The youth looked at his younger brother. "You comin'?"

"Sure am, I'm tired of gettin' beat by you."

They put the checkers away and Aaron looked over at their pa. "Come on, Pa. Let's get some sleep."

"I'll be along in a spell," Simon Peter said from behind the newspaper. "I just want to finish up this article they have in here 'bout them catchin' that no-good Booth."

"It's almost a mercy they brought him in dead," Daniel said as the boys headed out the door. "It spares Mrs. Lincoln the pain of a trial."

Simon Peter nodded gravely. "They talk about the president's funeral in here, too. You oughta be goin' since you served in the war and all."

"I'd like to, but I don't want to leave you shorthanded."

"We've been doin' just fine. Almost got you caught up to where you should be this time o' year."

Daniel opened his mouth to reply when Adele, aided by Mary, came into the room. Daniel immediately took her from his aunt and helped her sit next to him on the sofa.

"She heard you talking and wanted to come downstairs," Mary said. She settled down in a small rocker next to Katherine.

"Is Jacob better?" Daniel asked hopefully.

"His fever's broken," his aunt said with a smile. "And his hand is beginning to heal."

"Thank the Lord," Daniel said and embraced Adele.

"I heard what Simon Peter said as we were coming down

the stairs," Mary said, and he turned his attention to her. "He's right. You should go."

"Yes, Daniel, you should go and see President Lincoln one last time," Adele said. "I wish I could go, but I do not think I am strong enough." She looked over at Katherine, and Daniel watched as the young widow gathered herself to speak to her. "Perhaps you should go with Daniel. . .Miss Wallace."

Katherine looked up, startled. "Oh, well. . ."

"I know she would like to go, Adele, but that may not be the best idea," Daniel said. Katherine had expressed a desire to say good-bye to the president a few days ago, but she knew her accent made it impossible. And there was the distinct possibility that someone would recognize her. A number of people from Ostrander would more than likely be going down. He said as much now. "I don't want to disrupt the viewing," he finished.

"He's right, ma'am," Simon Peter said. "Durin' the war down at Camp Chase they was lettin' some Confederate prisoners of war have the run of Columbus. Them officers behaved themselves, but folk down there didn't like it one bit. Almost had a riot down there one time."

"But I remember that day in the store when we all found out. Miss Wallace, you were so sad. And Mary tells me how you have always been faithful to the Union." Adele looked imploringly at Daniel. "What if she wears my mourning clothes? I have a spoon bonnet with a veil. It would hide her face."

Mary raised her eyebrows. "If she didn't speak it would work. And we could hem your dress. You're a bit taller than Katherine."

Adele nodded and looked at Daniel.

He glanced at Katherine.

"I'm not sure I really have any right to be there," she murmured.

"You're a citizen of this country, Katherine," Daniel said quietly. "You have as much right to be there as anyone in this room. Maybe more. You were faithful to the Union when all around others weren't."

"I have the idea President Lincoln would be very pleased to have someone from the South come pay their respects," Mary added.

Daniel watched her face as she thought it out. She finally nodded, if a bit reluctantly.

"Thank you kindly, Mrs. Stephens," she said.

Even though Katherine had tried to soften her accent, Daniel still saw a pained look flit across Adele's face. He knew she was making a concerted effort to let go of her blame and anger. It was encouraging to see the effort she now took to be kind to Katherine. But he knew she still was not comfortable with Katherine's accent. At least not yet.

To his disappointment Katherine rose. "I'm going to bed." She looked over at Mary. "Do you want me to check on Jacob?"

"No, he's sleeping peacefully," she replied as she looked at Katherine worriedly. "Are you sure you're not coming down with something?"

"No, I'm fine." She turned to the rest of them. "Good night."

Daniel rose and followed her to the stairs. "Katherine."

She stopped and turned her head slightly. "I'm sorry, Daniel. I really am tired."

"I won't keep you then, but I want a chance to talk to you privately. Soon."

She nodded and quickly continued up the stairs. As he watched her go, he wondered if he had been wrong to think she cared for him.

❧

Katherine lay in bed a long time before she fell asleep. A certain degree of guilt had been lifted from her shoulders since Daniel had told her about how Nate had died. At least she need not feel so awful at the very sight of Adele Stephens. But leaving was becoming more and more tempting in spite of what the Lord was telling her. How could anyone around here heal if she were here?

And besides, it was very clear to her now that Daniel had feelings for the young widow. She should have seen it before.

Her hand flew to her jaw and tears pricked at her eyes. *Father, I told You this would happen. I can't stay. I have to find a way back to. . .South Carolina.* She couldn't bring herself to say home. South Carolina would never truly be her home again. No matter where she was, her heart would always be in Ohio. She loved the crispness of the air and soft chirping of the crickets in the evening, the rush of Mill Creek and the gentle gaze of Daniel's soft green eyes.

Tears fell free and fast down her face, making her pillow damp. She'd dream about him again tonight. She dreamed about him almost every night since that day he'd found her crying by the creek. It had confused her at first, but it didn't take long for her to figure out it was because she loved him.

She flung her arm over her face, begging God to let her leave. Her heart went back and forth with Him for quite some time. By the time she fell asleep she had promised Him she would do nothing. For now.

fourteen

Early Saturday morning, Daniel stood in the parlor waiting for Katherine to come down. He was in full dress uniform with a black band on his left arm and a fringed black sash attached to his sword hilt. According to the newspapers, all officers not on duty had been invited to participate in the proceedings, but Daniel had not been interested. He would have had to report to Tod Barracks down in Columbus at six o'clock this morning, which would have been impractical since Katherine was coming with him.

Soft movement caused him to turn and see Katherine standing in the doorway of the parlor. Normally he couldn't bear to see a woman in mourning. He hated seeing his aunt perpetually dressed in black and he was glad Katherine, as she was not related to his family, did not have to wear the somber color in remembrance of his mother. But the darkness of Adele's dress set off her eyes and brought out the red highlights in her auburn hair.

Neither one of them said anything for a minute or two.

Finally Daniel spoke. "I must look ridiculous in this," he half joked as he rested his hand on his sword.

"Oh no," she said quickly. "You look quite. . .military." She flushed and looked down.

Daniel had the idea she was going to say a very different word, and he wished once more that it would just be the two of them driving to Delaware. He dearly wanted to be certain of what she was feeling.

Daniel had decided to drive into Delaware to catch the train rather than getting on in Ostrander where someone might recognize Katherine. Professor Harris had very graciously offered to look after Scioto and the carriage while they were in Columbus. Jeremiah, another one of Simon Peter's sons, was in charge of the professor's stables and had come to ride with them into Delaware.

Mary came into the room just then and fussed a little with Katherine's frock. "For having so little time, Adele did a good job," she commented as she stood back to look at her.

"Yes," she replied, looking down at the hem. "I'm glad nothing had to be done to the bodice."

Daniel saw Jeremiah waiting for them in the drive. "We'd better go."

Mary handed Katherine the spoon bonnet with its heavy black veil.

Taking it, Katherine embraced her friend and looked at her worriedly. "Will you be all right without me?"

"I'll be just fine," the older woman reassured her. "Simon Peter and the boys will be back as soon as they've seen the funeral train go by." Those who couldn't make it to any of the cities where the president would lie in state were congregating by railroad crossings where his train would pass to pay their respects. Mary turned and hugged her nephew. "Take good care of her."

Daniel smiled. "You know I will."

❧

The sun shone brightly down on the city of Columbus as long lines of people filled the sidewalk along High Street to view the body of President Abraham Lincoln, which now lay in the rotunda of the Ohio statehouse.

Daniel and Katherine were among them, quietly inching their way forward toward Capitol Square. Their train had arrived in Columbus at nine thirty, over two hours after the president's body had arrived in the capital city.

A procession had already taken him through a preplanned route around the statehouse before delivering him to lie in state inside. The doors would close, they had heard, at six o'clock that evening in order for the body to move on to Indianapolis.

The crowds were so immense Daniel had worried they might not get a chance to see him. But his army uniform caught a good deal of attention, and several people asked why he had not taken part in the procession. Each time he was asked, Daniel had nodded toward Katherine, who was holding his arm, and explained he was escorting a young lady whose only brother had died in the war. As a result people insisted they go ahead of them. Daniel had protested at first, but most people were so vehement in their insistence his objections fell on deaf ears. It had happened so frequently they were now approaching the statehouse far sooner than they would have been. Daniel had given up trying to stop their heartfelt gestures.

Katherine, on the other hand, despaired, hating to fool so many good people. The last time it had happened she had given Daniel a look of dismay, hoping he would look at her long enough to make out her face through the veil.

He had pulled her close. "It's true enough, isn't it?" he asked.

"Yes, but—"

"Don't say anything. I won't have something happening to you." The look on his face made her dizzy, and she grasped his arm tightly as they walked on.

She looked around and tried to turn her attention to something else. The statehouse was now well within view, and Katherine studied it as they slowly moved along.

South Carolina had begun work on its statehouse when she was eleven, and she had seen the incomplete building in Columbia several times. It had promised to be a grand structure.

But by the beginning of the war it had only been partially complete, and over the course of the conflict construction had ground almost to a halt. Whether or not it had survived the burning of Columbia she could not say.

Ohio's statehouse was similar in style, but it had a quiet elegance which she found she preferred. Rather than a large imposing dome topped with a spire, a large drumlike cupola with windows all around sat atop the rectangular structure. The building sat on a square surrounded by a wrought iron fence with a green lawn at each corner.

Daniel had told her there were four entryways, each facing a different direction on the compass. They were drawing near the west entrance now. Black cloth was wrapped around the massive Grecian pillars in front of the doors, and black bunting graced each of the eight windows on either side.

The fence was broken by a gateway over which a sign had been hung. It read: OHIO MOURNS.

She glanced at Daniel. A weight had settled over him ever since the statehouse had come into view. As he read the sign his face became graver.

As they moved beneath the gate another sign had been hung directly above the pillars: WITH MALICE TOWARD NONE; WITH CHARITY FOR ALL. Katherine recalled Rev. Warren quoting the phrase from President Lincoln's second inaugural address.

They climbed the broad limestone stairway and passed between the pillars to face one last sign which hung directly over the heavy double doors: GOD MOVES IN A MYSTERIOUS WAY. Daniel stopped and stared at it.

A gap opened in front of them, and after another second or two a gentleman behind them gently coughed. Katherine grasped Daniel's hand, and he looked at her as if he had just woken from a dream. Seeing the break in front of them, he quickly escorted her forward. A short hallway was before them with another small flight of steps leading up into the rotunda.

Katherine's heart pounded as she realized she would soon be looking at the face of her fallen president. She glanced down at the basket on her arm, wondering if she would be brave enough to do all she had planned. Mary had packed them food for their lunch and dinner, and at the last moment Katherine had included a small spray of violets to put on or near the president's coffin. She had been sure enough of the gesture earlier, but now she felt unaccountably shy. *Father, help me be bold.*

They climbed the last step into the rotunda. Katherine looked around her. The walls of the round room were draped in black, broken only by four arched entryways and a painting labeled "Perry's Victory on Lake Erie."

She looked up. Sunshine shone down through the pretty stained glass dome and bathed the solemn scene with light. The entire room smelled of various flowers, the scent of lilacs being the most prominent.

A black carpeted platform appeared at her feet. The line of four abreast split here as two people on each side walked up the platform to view the president. Daniel let go of her arm and she allowed him to approach the coffin first as she reached into the basket for her spray of flowers.

They stood there for a moment, both of them taking in the still face of President Abraham Lincoln. Katherine stared at the still yet kindly face and tears sprang to her eyes. She sent up a silent prayer for the great man's widow and children.

Daniel rubbed his right hand and his jaw was clenched tight. He moved on a second later, and Katherine followed but not before swiftly laying the violets at the base of the coffin. Daniel had turned to help her step off the platform and saw her gesture. He threaded his fingers through her own as they left the rotunda and followed the rest of the crowd out through the north entrance.

❧

The line of people broke up once they exited the statehouse, and Daniel walked Katherine off to the side. The sight of his fallen leader and Katherine's sweet gesture had moved him greatly, and he hoped she wouldn't let go of his hand until he had taken a moment to collect himself.

She didn't; rather, she laid her other hand over their clasped ones. He wished he could see her face and her eyes, which he knew were probably soft with sympathy and her own unshed tears.

He squeezed her small hand. "Thank you," he whispered. Looking closely he could just make out through the veil her small smile and a tear rolling down her cheek. While he took out his pocket watch to check the time, she wiped it away with her handkerchief. "It's nearly three and there's supposed to be an oration on the East Lawn," he offered.

She nodded her approval and they made their way over.

A great number of people had already gathered, and Daniel could not get them very close to the platform which had been erected in front of the east entrance of the statehouse. But he knew they would be well within earshot of the speakers, provided they spoke loudly enough.

People closed in around them, and he and Katherine had to stand quite close to one another. He therefore allowed himself the luxury of placing his arm around her small waist to keep her from being jostled.

He glanced down and saw he was close enough to make out her face quite clearly through the veil. Dark lashes lay against her pale cheeks and she didn't return his gaze.

Tearing his eyes away he watched the dignitaries step up onto the platform. He immediately recognized Major General Joseph Hooker, who had once commanded the Army of the

Potomac, along with several other generals. A military band played a dirge, and a choral selection was sung before a prayer was offered up.

The state senator from Chillicothe, the Honorable Job E. Stevenson, rose and began to speak. "Ohio mourns, America mourns," he said. "The civilized world will mourn the cruel death of Abraham Lincoln, the brave, the wise, the good; bravest, wisest, best of men."

The crowd was deathly silent as State Senator Stevenson spoke. He summarized President Lincoln's life, his rise to office, his steadfast service during the war, and the forgiveness he offered the South in his last inaugural address. "But he is slain," he then declared. "Slain by slavery."

Daniel looked around as more than a few people began to murmur and nod.

"That fiend incarnate did the deed. Beaten in battle, the leaders sought to save slavery by assassination." The murmurs grew louder as State Senator Stevenson continued and several people shouted as he declared the souls of murdered Union soldiers would rise up in judgment against the South. "Let us beware the Delilah of the South, who has so lately betrayed our strong man. Let the 'Prodigals' feed on the husks till they come in repentance, and ask to be received in their father's house—not as the equals to their faithful brethren but on a level with their former servants."

Katherine swayed and Daniel looked down at her in alarm. Even through the veil he could see how pale she was, and he moved her through the crowd until they came to an open area of the lawn near the north exit.

She leaned heavily against him for a moment before raising her face to his. "Oh Daniel, I can't stay," she whispered tearfully.

He grasped her by the arms and pulled her close. "You *can't* go."

fifteen

"Why?" Katherine whispered and then caught her breath at the look on Daniel's face. As she gazed into his soft green eyes a sharp thrill shot through her chest. In the back of her mind something told her if it wasn't for the veil and their current surroundings. . . The thought made her dizzy and she grasped the front of his jacket for support.

People glanced at them as they passed and his grip quickly loosened. "Come on," he said deeply as he slipped her hand into the crook of his arm. "We should start heading back toward the train station."

Katherine gripped his arm tightly as they moved through the busy city streets. She didn't dare put into conscious thought what she had seen in his eyes. She still wasn't quite sure she could believe it.

What about Adele? He'd seemed so attentive to the young widow the past several days. But then Katherine's thoughts swung to the way he would look at her and the way he'd held her in the parlor the day he brought Adele and Jacob to the farm. And he said he wanted to talk to her. Alone. She had assumed it would be a confession of what he was feeling for Adele, so she'd planned on making every effort to avoid him. Now she wasn't so sure.

The train ride back to Delaware was crowded, and they were both happy to get out into the fresh evening air. Jeremiah was waiting with the carriage and Scioto at the station, and they drove him back to Professor Harris's home before going on their way.

Dusk was setting in as they journeyed home. It was nearly an hour between Delaware and the farm, plenty of time to talk.

Katherine buried her hands in the folds of her dress, clenched tightly so Daniel wouldn't see how they shook. Her heart felt like a drum. It wasn't that she was afraid of Daniel—far, *far* from it—but this was a situation she had never faced in all her life. What was she supposed to do? What if she were wrong? What if she were right? The latter thought caused a thrill to run straight through to her fingertips. As her mind whirled in nervous confusion, Daniel spoke and she nearly jumped clean out of her skin.

"You can probably take off the bonnet now," he said.

Her heart raced so fast she began to feel ill. She glanced at him. "Don't—don't you think I should wait until after Bellepoint?"

Bellepoint was east of the farm and Elijah Carr did a good deal of business in the town. When they had rode through that morning, Daniel told her to be sure to keep her face hidden. He now gave her a funny look and shrugged. "Most people will be turned in by the time we ride through. And I'm sure Carr is home by now. His farm isn't even within sight of the road."

"Well, best be safe than sorry," she murmured.

He gave her a slightly bemused, knowing look but said nothing in reply.

Even when they were well past Bellepoint, Katherine couldn't bring herself to even lift the bonnet's veil much less take it off. She fussed and fidgeted, avoiding Daniel's gaze. Fortunately, he said nothing and they rode the rest of the way home in silence.

It was dark by the time they reached the house. When Katherine attempted to get out of the carriage, the thickness of the veil nearly caused her to fall out. She felt Daniel take her by the arms and settle her safely on the ground.

His voice was filled with tender amusement as he spoke to her. "Katherine, take that silly thing off before you break your pretty little neck."

With shaking hands she removed the pins and untied the hat, laying it aside on the carriage seat. She turned around to find him standing very close to her, and it was difficult to keep a straight thought in her head. Looking past him she noticed the house was dark. "Oh," she breathed. "They must have turned in."

His eyes never left her. "Well, it is late."

Katherine stared at the ground. Her heart had begun its furious pounding again, and she hid her hands in the folds of her skirt.

Daniel lifted her chin with a gentle finger and she was forced to look at him. Moonlight danced in his green eyes as his hand cupped her face. "I've been wanting to talk to you." His voice was deep and soft.

As his thumb stroked her cheek, Katherine found herself reaching out to hold on to him. Her legs had suddenly become quite weak. She felt his hand slide around her waist, pulling her closer still. "What did you want to say?" she murmured.

"Only this," he whispered as his lips brushed hers.

Katherine's hands quickly wrapped themselves around his broad shoulders and the kiss deepened. This was what she'd been dreaming about.

Of course! This was all a dream. She'd wake up within the next few seconds like she always did and find nothing in her arms but a pillow. But instead of waking up, she found Daniel had lifted his head to look at her with such tenderness it was all she could do to not cry.

"Now do you understand why you can't go?"

She nodded. Breathless, she buried her head in his chest for a moment. "Why. . .why did you call me pretty?"

His lips brushed the top of her head. "Why shouldn't I?" he whispered.

Her voice shook as she answered. "Oh, Daniel, I'm not. I'm just this drab little. . .nothing."

"No. Don't even think that." The firmness of his voice caused her to look up and meet his gaze. "You are the most beautiful woman I've ever met, and not just here," he said, brushing his thumb across her cheek once more. "Your sweet spirit shines through everything you say and do. Especially through your incredible eyes."

"Incredible? *My* eyes?" she gasped, unable to believe what she was hearing. "You've *seen* my eyes, haven't you?"

"On more than one occasion." He smiled.

"You must have taken leave of your senses then, Daniel Kirby! My eyes are the least—" Before she could say more he was tenderly kissing her again.

"I could lose myself in your eyes for the rest of my life," he finally murmured, making a point of gazing into them for a long while before he spoke again. "I love you, Katherine Wallace."

She stared at him. "This is one of the nicest dreams I've ever had."

"You think you're dreaming?" he asked incredulously.

"I must be. In half a minute it'll be morning and I'll wake up to have you tell me you're really in love with Adele."

"Adele?" He laughed. "Adele is like a sister to me. What I feel for her is nothing like what I feel for you." Daniel bent his head to kiss her once more when they both caught sight of a soft light coming from the parlor window. "I guess Aunt Mary waited up after all." He placed a lingering kiss on her forehead before stepping away to lead Scioto and the carriage to the barn.

Katherine watched him, dazed, before remembering herself. Since this was all a dream, she might as well tell him how she felt. She'd woken up too soon all the other times. "Daniel!"

He was back beside her in an instant. "What?"

"Oh. . .I know I'm only dreaming. I love you."

"You're not dreaming." He smiled and reached up to stroke her cheek. "I'll prove you wrong in the morning."

"I dearly hope so."

sixteen

Daniel stepped out of the barn the next morning, having finished the chores and dressed for church, when he caught sight of Katherine on her way to the henhouse. She walked in before he could get her attention and he decided to wait for her.

He leaned against the whitewashed clapboard with a pounding heart. He remembered how deeply Nate had loved Adele and the affection his parents had for one another, but he never really expected to find love himself. Instead he had seen himself remaining a bachelor like Professor Harris. Not for lack of prospects of course. A number of girls from Ohio Wesleyan's female college had chased after him, and he had courted a couple of them. But the relationships hadn't lasted; he'd been far too interested in his studies and the young ladies too interested in catching a husband.

But Katherine was different. Daniel found in her someone who would willingly join him in his studies. She didn't sigh and look bored when he spoke of poetry or mythology. She had a passion for learning and, more importantly, a passion for the Lord.

He reached into his pocket and pulled out a small leather pouch, tipping the small gold ring it contained into his palm. Aunt Mary had given him his mother's wedding ring the day after he'd come home, and he'd carried it with him ever since. The morning sun glinted off the golden crisscrossing lines along the band, an Irish pattern. It had been in the Kirby family for generations.

Just then one of the cows lowed and he frowned. *You're a farmer now,* he thought as he returned the heirloom to his pocket. What right did he have offering her that kind of life? Oh, she seemed contented enough, but could he be satisfied knowing she would be far better suited as a professor's wife?

The henhouse door opened and Daniel deliberately pushed the thought aside. He was eager to prove to her that his declaration last night hadn't been a dream.

Katherine set down a heavy basket of eggs, and as she turned to close the door, he grasped her hand and pulled her into his arms. Before she could say a word he was kissing her, slowly and deeply.

"Daniel Aaron Kirby!" she gasped weakly. "Mary will see."

"Right now I don't care if the entire state of Ohio sees us or hears me telling you how much I love you." His arms tightened around her. "Still believe it's a dream?"

Her eyes softened and she bit her lip as a shy smile crept over her face. "No," she whispered.

It was all he could do to not kiss her again. Instead he let her go and, picking up the basket of eggs, took her hand. "Come on. I'll walk you in." He relished the feel of her fingers entwined with his, and as they walked he caught her glancing at him. "What?"

"You're wearing your uniform again."

The admiring look in her eyes gave him such a rush he almost forgot to answer. "I thought it was only proper to wear this to services until the president is laid to rest later this week." He stopped and she looked at him questioningly. "Come to church this morning."

"Daniel, I shouldn't," she replied, looking away.

"You've never really explained why you feel you have to do this," he said. "You know it's only going to take longer for them to heal and accept you."

"Is it? Seems to me the less they see of me—"

"The less they'll think about what they need to be doing, which is accepting you because you're their sister in Christ. Being Southern should have nothing to do with it." He pulled her forward and kissed her on the forehead. "Do you know what Adele told me?"

"What?"

"She said being around you is helping her let go of the pain and anger she's been feeling."

"She blamed me for Nate's death," she murmured.

"She did. But your example has shown her what she needs to do. Don't you think that's what you should do for the people at Mill Creek Church?"

She opened her mouth to answer, but Mary called to them from the kitchen door. "Will you two be joining us for breakfast?"

Inside, as they sat down at the table, Daniel noticed that Adele was wearing a dress of pale blue, the skirt being held out by numerous petticoats. Her hair was pulled neatly back in a chignon and she looked almost like her old self. "Are you coming with Aunt Mary and me this morning, Adele?" he asked.

Adele and his aunt looked at each other. Mary was dressed in simple work clothes. "No, Daniel," Adele replied calmly. "I intend to go to church with you and Miss Wallace this morning."

He heard Katherine drop her fork and looked to see her staring wide eyed at the young widow. "Oh, Mrs. Stephens, I've promised—"

"Katherine, this staying away from services is nonsense," Mary said firmly. "If you eat quickly you can get yourself into something suitable before you three need to leave. I'll stay and tend to Jacob. He needs a few days more yet."

Daniel could tell by the sound of his aunt's voice she was going to brook no refusal. And from the stricken look on Katherine's little face he knew she knew it as well.

She rose. "I'm. . .not really hungry. I think I'll change now," she muttered, sweeping from the room.

He looked after her, frustrated he couldn't go hold her and tell her everything would be all right.

A warm hand found his and he turned to see a sweet, knowing smile on Adele's face.

"Let me go speak with her," she said gently before rising from her seat and following Katherine.

⁊⁊

Katherine sat on her bed, still dressed in her work clothes and staring at her dresses hanging in the simple walnut wardrobe. She couldn't quite decide which dress was proper for a lamb being led to the slaughter to wear. The swish of petticoats caused her to look up and meet Adele's gentle smile.

"Such lovely dresses," Adele said as she swept over to the wardrobe door.

"Thank you," Katherine muttered. "Mary and I altered a few of hers. There's only one that's new." She and Mary had only managed to make one dress for her since their arrival. It was a pretty day dress with a rosette print and a background of deep blue.

Adele immediately reached for it. "I will tell you a secret. In spite of how I felt, I always liked this on you. You must wear it and we will be a pretty pair as we sit together this morning." She saw the terrible look on Katherine's face and, becoming more serious, the young widow sat down beside her. "This is not right. They will not come to accept you if you are not there."

"That's what Daniel said."

"He is right, you know."

"I know it's just. . ." Katherine paused and looked back up at Adele. "Am I truly helping you to heal?"

A strained look crossed the young widow's face and she placed her hand over Katherine's. "If you had not come here, I would have drowned in my hate. I would have grown into a bitter old woman and died far from God."

"But you've been attending church."

"Only for the sake of my son." Adele squeezed her hand. "And going to church does not make you close to Him, you know." She placed her free hand over her heart. "You must have and know Him here."

Katherine nodded. She had attended services many times with her family but it had only been for the sake of appearances. The words of their reverend had not touched their hearts as they had hers. "But how could I have possibly been an example to you? I've hardly seen you."

"But I have seen you. You treated my son with much kindness, and I would watch you during services and I knew how patiently you accepted how people treated you. May would tell me."

"May?" Katherine asked hopefully.

"Yes, she is a dear young lady, and she likes you very much."

"Her parents certainly don't," Katherine replied sadly.

"They are good people," Adele reassured her. "Do not think too badly of them. I hope you will come to know them as I do." She smiled. "Now you must get dressed. Your Daniel is waiting for us I am sure."

Katherine blushed, happy and shy at the same time. "Mrs. Stephens—"

"If we are to be friends you must call me Adele."

Katherine's throat went tight. "Then, I hope you will call me Katherine."

Adele's smile broadened and she leaned toward her. "We

will go together and sit side by side. If anyone wants to say something, they will say it to me."

Whatever courage she had taken from Adele's words melted away at the first shocked look she got when the three of them walked up to the church door.

Daniel seemed to sense her discomfort and looked down at her. "It'll be all right."

Her heart flipped at the look he gave her and she squeezed his arm tighter. She had no notion how she had managed to win the heart of such a good and handsome man. Katherine pressed her lips together at the sweet memory of his kiss this morning. No, last night hadn't been a dream.

A great deal of murmuring and pointing went on as they sat down in a pew near the front. Adele smiled calmly and greeted a few people who answered her back in stunned voices. Katherine sat down beside her and immediately reached for a hymnal. She didn't look up until the end of the opening song when she felt Daniel slide away from her. Startled, she saw none other than May Decker daintily stepping in front of him, settling herself next to her with a barely suppressed smile. Katherine began to panic. May's parents would be furious that she had not returned to sit with them after playing the opening hymn.

Adele took her hand then and Katherine turned to see Rev. Warren step up to the lectern. A small smile was on his face, and he gave her the barest of winks as he bid them all to open to the book of Galatians.

Services slipped by more quickly than Katherine had ever remembered. May rose all too soon to play the closing hymn, and afterward the room was deathly quiet. Within a few minutes people began to stand awkwardly, yet still not saying much of anything.

Unabashed, Adele rose, pulling Katherine along with her.

Linking her arm through hers the young widow started to walk her down the aisle, Daniel and May not far behind. Katherine nearly gasped when she saw Mrs. Warren approaching them with Ruth Decker quickly coming up behind her.

"Adele," Mrs. Warren exclaimed, "how nice to see you." She glanced hesitantly at Katherine.

"Thank you, Mrs. Warren. It is good to see you as well." She smiled pleasantly. "Is it not good that Miss Wallace was able to come this morning?"

Mrs. Warren seemed to hesitate and Ruth Decker now spoke up. "Adele Stephens, you can't be serious. She's a secesh."

Katherine felt Daniel move behind her, and she reached back to lay a hand on his arm. His eyes were dark with anger, but he took heed of her imploring look and said nothing.

"Miss Wallace is not a secesh," Adele declared calmly. "She is a sister in Christ. I am ashamed to say I have not always seen her that way, but over the past month she has shown me that God tells us to love our enemies, not so we can heap coals upon their heads but so we might learn to love them." She looked around at the other members of the congregation who stood watching the little scene play out. "We have all lost much. Brothers, sons. . .husbands." Her voice shook on the last word and Katherine squeezed her hand in sympathy. "But I will not allow myself to lose my faith as well. I will accept Miss Wallace as my sister in Christ."

"And so will I," May declared.

Ruth Decker seemed completely thunderstruck, but Mrs. Warren stepped toward Katherine and took both her hands in hers. Her face was awash with shame and tears began to fall from her eyes. Rev. Warren came to stand next to his wife as she spoke. "Miss Wallace, I am so sorry. When Paul told me we needed to accept you, I couldn't. . ."

Katherine gently squeezed her hands. "Mrs. Warren, please

don't give it another thought. Your husband told us about your nephew and I am so terribly sorry."

She glanced over at Ruth Decker, who had backed off and looked very uncertain. Mr. Decker stood beside her and gave her a tentative smile. Without hesitation Katherine walked up to the woman and smiled gently. "Mrs. Decker, I never got to thank you for your kindness and hospitality when Mary and I first arrived. Thank you kindly."

Ruth Decker burst into tears and caught Katherine up in a firm embrace. "I am so ashamed of myself," she sobbed. "I can be so ridiculous at times. There's no possible excuse for how I acted."

"That's all right, Mrs. Decker. Don't worry yourself. I hope we can be friends now."

"Oh of course," Ruth exclaimed as she released her and mopped at her eyes with a handkerchief. "I'm going to have a quilting bee very soon, and you and Mary and Adele must come."

There were other apologies after that. Not as many as Katherine would have liked but, she mused as they rode home, it was a good beginning.

Adele grasped her hand and they smiled at each other. "I am looking forward to the quilting bee," she said.

"I am, too," Katherine replied. "Mary and I having been working on a quilt, but it won't be ready for a while yet."

A gleam appeared in Adele's eye and she threw a quick glance at Daniel who was sitting in the seat in front of them, driving. "A Double Wedding Ring pattern perhaps?" she asked in a hushed voice.

Katherine clapped a hand over her mouth to stifle her gasp. "Adele!" she hissed.

The young widow's eyes danced but she said no more.

Katherine was glad to see her so cheerful, a stark contrast to how she must have been feeling a mere week ago. She glanced up at her new friend.

"If you had not come here I would have drowned in my hate. . . ."

"Your example has shown her what she needs to do."

Adele's and Daniel's voices echoed in her mind and suddenly coming here made sense. She remembered the day Mary had told her she was going to abandon her plantation and go home to Ohio. The urge to go with her was so strong she had felt sure it was God Himself guiding her.

The anxiety and worry she had felt for the past two months vanished as she now recognized her part in His plan. That God had used her as an instrument of healing gave her a sense of confidence she hadn't felt for a long while. Not since before all that had happened with Chloe.

She fingered her scar thoughtfully. *Will I ever find out what happened to her, Father?*

Daniel had written his friend as he had promised, but the man had been unable to find out anything.

Her hand dropped away from her face and she squared her jaw resolutely. *Trust Him,* she told herself. *Don't lean on your own understanding.*

They pulled up the Kirbys' drive and Adele immediately climbed out. Katherine knew she was eager to see how Jacob was. The boy was weak but Mary had declared he would be fine after a few days of rest.

Adele was in the house even before Daniel had a chance to help Katherine out of the carriage. His fingers wrapped around hers as he helped her step to the ground, and her heart did a double flip as he pulled her close and placed a quick kiss on her lips. "You were wonderful this morning," he murmured.

She smiled and was about to reply when they heard the door to the house open. They turned to see Adele standing there, her face deeply distressed.

Katherine felt Daniel's arms tense. "What is it, Adele?" he

asked. "Is it Jacob?"

She quickly shook her head. "Katherine has a visitor."

Katherine stared at her in surprise. "Who?"

"You must come inside," she replied stiffly before disappearing into the house.

The look on Adele's face so upset her she was up the steps and into the house before Daniel. At the door to the parlor she gasped.

A gaunt man dressed in Confederate gray stood in front of the sofa where Mary and Adele sat looking at him. He turned to Katherine and she was shocked to hear her brother's voice come from the skeletal form. "Gather your things, Katherine. I've come to fetch you home."

seventeen

The soldier in Daniel immediately reached for his Colt the instant he saw Confederate gray. He cocked the weapon as he moved to stand in front of Katherine.

The Southern officer glared at him. "You would shoot an unarmed man, sir?"

Daniel hesitated. Glancing at the man's belt, he saw his holster was indeed empty. "No," he replied as he slowly uncocked his weapon and lowered it.

Katherine moved to go around him, but he blocked her with his arm, causing the soldier's glare to intensify. She laid a hand on his arm and Daniel looked down at her. "It's all right," she said. "It's my brother, Charles."

Daniel reluctantly let her go by.

She started to hug her brother. When he did not return the embrace, she hastily stepped back a bit, hands clasped together. "Charles, I'm so glad to see you're alive. Aunt Ada and I found your name posted on the lists. Where have you been all this time?"

"An unfortunate clerical error. I've been a guest of the Union army for the past eight months," he replied, glaring at Daniel.

Daniel held his tongue but watched him carefully.

"The last three were at Camp Chase. I was released just yesterday. Had I not been wounded, I would have written sooner to tell you and Aunt Ada I was alive. When I finally was able to, she told me how you had abandoned her to come here."

Katherine pursed her lips slightly but her gaze did not waver

141

from her brother for a moment.

Mary broke the silence which had settled over the room. "You look so thin, Charles," she said gently. "Let me get you something to eat."

"No thank you, ma'am." Charles's polite words were offset by the sneer on his face. "I have only come to take my sister home." He looked piercingly at Katherine. "Her fiancé is waiting for her."

Daniel's eyes widened as Katherine gasped. "Charles, what do you mean? I was never engaged."

"You are now. Aunt Ada has it all arranged. You will finally bring prestige to our name with your marriage to Thaddeus Adams."

"Charles, you can't be serious!" Mary exclaimed. "Thaddeus Adams is nearly three times her age."

"You will kindly stay out of this." Charles snapped. "This is a family matter and no concern of yours."

"Don't talk to her that way. She's been more like family to me than you ever were, Charles."

Daniel stared at Katherine in surprise. This was a new side to her, so unlike the meek, soft-spoken woman he'd come to know. But as much as he loved her gentle ways, he was glad to see her more assertive and sure of herself. And he did not fail to notice she wasn't even reaching for her scar, as she certainly would have before. He silently cheered her on as she defiantly glared up at her older brother who was nearly as tall as he was.

Taking a deep breath and calming herself, she went on. "I'm sorry, but I won't even consider leaving here to marry Mr. Adams. Ohio is my home now."

Her brother's face grew red. "As head of our family, you are under my protection," he shot back. "You will do as I say."

"No!"

Charles's face contorted with rage as he backhanded

Katherine across the jaw.

As she crumpled to the floor, Daniel sprang forward and pinned Charles Wallace against the wall, his pistol pointed directly between his eyes. Suddenly Daniel wasn't in his family's parlor but on a smoke-filled battlefield, his enemy backed up against a bullet-riddled stump. He cocked his gun.

"Daniel!"

He jumped at the warm hand on his arm and blinked as the image melted away.

Adele was standing next to him, the pressure from her hands growing as she tried to force him to lower his weapon. Mary knelt on the floor next to Katherine, who he desperately hoped was only unconscious.

He swallowed and backed away but kept his Colt trained on Charles. "Get out," he said roughly. "Get off my property and don't come back. If anyone's going to marry your sister, it'll be me."

❧

Adele and Mary made Katherine stay in bed for several days. She tried to tell them she was fine, but Mary would have none of it.

"Head injuries are nothing to be played with," she'd said sternly on the second day. "Your head hit the floor awfully hard when you fell."

Katherine remembered Charles backhanding her but little else after that save for the vague yet pleasant memory of Daniel carrying her up the stairs.

By the fourth day she still had a large lump on the back of her head and her jaw was bruised and tender, but she felt more than ready to get out of bed. She missed Daniel terribly. Mary would not permit him to even come up the stairs, but the notes he'd been sending up had lessened the ache considerably.

The first had been a word-for-word copy of four of

Shakespeare's sonnets: eighteen, twenty-nine, fifty-five, and fifty-seven. How had he known those had always been her favorites? The next evening she had blushed furiously over a copy of Byron's "She Walks in Beauty."

Now, as she sat up in bed rereading one of the sonnets, a small dark head poked its way around the corner of her door. "Jacob!" she exclaimed softly and motioned for him to come in.

She was happy to see he was up and dressed and his once-infected hand seemed back to normal. It was still wrapped snugly with clean strips of linen. Mary was taking no chances of its becoming infected again.

He sat on the edge of her bed and picked up one of the sonnets. She smiled as the child read the poem, his face becoming more confused by the second.

"What does 'bootless cries' mean?" he asked. "Is he crying 'cause he lost his boots?"

Katherine chuckled. "No, he's sad because his cries seem meaningless."

"Oh," he said, handing it back. He looked at her for a minute and frowned. "That man was mean to hit you. Who was he?"

Katherine's heart was in her throat at the thought the boy had witnessed such violence. "Oh, Jacob, I'm sorry you saw that. Why were you even down there?"

"I heard someone talk mean to Mrs. O'Neal so I went downstairs so I could tell him to leave her alone." He smiled crookedly. "But you did that real good."

"What else did you see?" Katherine was eager to know what happened after everything went black. She had asked Adele and Mary how they had gotten Charles to leave, but they had simply urged her to rest, smiling mysteriously when they assured her he would not be back.

"Mr. Kirby, he slammed the man against the wall and pulled his gun on him."

Katherine gasped and her hands flew to her mouth. *Oh surely Daniel didn't shoot Charles!*

Seeing the look on her face, the boy hurried on. "But Ma talked to him and he backed off and told the man to get out." A broad smile lit up the youngster's face. "And then Mr. Kirby said if—"

"Jacob." They looked up to see Adele standing in the doorway, giving her son a look of gentle reproach. "You should not be bothering Miss Wallace. She needs her rest."

"Oh Adele," Katherine said as the woman took her son's seat after shooing him out. "I feel fine."

The young widow looked at her carefully. "What did my son tell you?"

"Daniel didn't really pull his gun on Charles, did he?"

Adele nodded soberly. "I have never seen Daniel so angry. For a moment it seemed he was someplace else. He was startled when I put my hand on his arm."

"Is he all right?"

She smiled reassuringly. "He seems fine. You can see for yourself. Mary says you may come down in a little while." Her eyes sparkled as she pulled a note from her dress pocket. "Daniel sends you this."

Katherine opened it and tears sprang to her eyes.

"Arise, my love, my fair one, and come away."
Song of Solomon 2:13

Mary came in a little later and helped Katherine get dressed. She was surprised when Mary laid out her blue dress and fussed over her nearly twenty minutes longer than necessary.

Putting her hair up in its usual style proved to be impossible; the lump on the back of her head was still so tender Mary was sure coiling braids against the nape of her neck would give her a headache. Instead she swept Katherine's thick hair up on either side, letting the rest fall in waves down to her waist.

Katherine looked at her nervously when she'd finished. She hadn't worn her hair down since she was a young girl. "Mary, I can't go down like this."

Mary smiled gently. "It's not entirely proper, but you won't be going out in public. You look just fine. Lovely, in fact."

Katherine winced at her choice of words and, glancing into the mirror in the door of her wardrobe, started.

Mary noticed and laid a hand on her arm. "What is it, dear?" she asked.

"I'm. . .pretty," she whispered. She closed her eyes and shook her head but nothing changed. The same attractive young lady was still staring back at her with large, expressive eyes and hair with fiery red highlights. "It must be the mirror or because my hair is down. . . ."

"Or because you've always been pretty?" Her friend pulled her into a warm hug. "Come on before Daniel wears a hole in the rug."

Mary left her at the foot of the stairs, sternly telling her she and Adele would not be very far away in the kitchen.

Katherine reached back and nervously patted her loose wavy hair once more before stepping into the parlor.

If she had somehow managed to become pretty in the course of four days then Daniel had become twice as handsome in the same amount of time. She barely breathed as he stopped his pacing to stare at her.

Before she knew it he was holding her tightly, like he would never let go.

❧

Daniel finally loosened his hold on Katherine and looked down at her. It was the first time he had seen her in days, and his eyes were instantly drawn to the ugly bruise Charles's blow had left on her jaw. Guilt gnawed at him as he ran his thumb over it.

Katherine's eyes softened. "It's not your fault," she said.

"I should have known better. You shouldn't have been within two feet of him."

"I'm fine," she soothed. "I've been through worse."

"And you'll never go through something like that ever again." He sealed his promise with a lingering kiss. Raising his head he noticed her hair. "Trying to start a new fashion?" he teased, holding up a handful of it.

"No." She blushed. "I still have quite a lump on the back of my head. Mary was worried if we put it up I'd have a frightful headache." The smile faded from her face and she took him in with worried eyes. "Adele said you weren't yourself after. . ." Her voice trailed off.

Daniel nodded and led her over to the sofa. "The war sneaks up on me at times," he said as they sat down.

Katherine's eyes grew large with worry. "It's not like Rev. Warren's nephew?"

"No," he quickly reassured her. "Nothing like that." Loud, sudden noises had a tendency to spook him more than they used to, and Michael had once awakened him from a very ugly dream. But he didn't feel like he wasn't in control or not getting on with life. "I was just so angry when he hit you. That and your brother and I being in uniform." He grasped her hands and squeezed them. "I doubt it will happen again."

"Do you want to talk about it with me?" she offered.

"Katherine, there are things I saw and experienced no woman should ever hear about," Daniel replied gravely. "But I've spoken with Michael several times." In spite of the fact he had not fought in the war, or perhaps because of it, Simon Peter's son was a considerate and careful listener. They had also prayed together on more than one occasion.

"I'll pray for you then," Katherine whispered tenderly.

He smiled as she squeezed his hands, and he glanced down at them. "Thank you. Just your presence is soothing. Like that first day out in the courtyard."

Her eyes dropped away and her cheeks turned crimson.

He was amazed by how beautiful she was when she was embarrassed. Some of her long, silky tresses fell over her shoulder. With her hair always pulled back in coiled braids he'd never had the opportunity to appreciate its dark, fiery depths. He gently pulled more of it over her shoulder and thought of the Byron poem he had copied for her. " 'And all that's best of dark and bright; Meet in her aspect and her eyes,'" he softly quoted. Their eyes met and he quickly found himself kissing her soft lips.

"Daniel Kirby," she reproached a moment later, "how scandalous of you to send me a poem from a man described—by his mistress no less—as 'mad, bad, and dangerous to know.'"

"Which is more scandalous, that I sent you one of his poems or that you know that about him?" They laughed and Daniel wanted nothing more than to spend the rest of his life going back and forth with her like this.

"Katherine. . ." His voice trailed off. The words were on the edge of his lips but he couldn't bring himself to say them. How could he? She wasn't meant for the kind of life he could offer her.

He quickly stood and she stared at him with startled eyes. "I'm sorry. I have to do something. Tell Aunt Mary I'll be back for dinner."

Daniel was so caught up with his own thoughts he failed to notice his aunt had followed him out to the barn and down to Scioto's stable.

He turned from fetching his saddle to find her standing

near the stairs with her arms crossed. Her lips were pursed slightly and she wore a look of concern. "What happened?" she asked him.

He glanced at her and quickly returned to saddling his horse. Both Adele and Aunt Mary had expected him to propose to Katherine this evening, especially after what they had heard him tell her brother. "I couldn't do it."

"Why? Katherine loves you dearly. I never saw her this way, even with Thomas."

"No, it's not her. It's me." He took Scioto's bridle off its hook and fiddled with the straps. "She deserves better than this."

His aunt didn't pretend to not understand what he meant. "She's perfectly content here, Daniel. I can assure you of that."

"Maybe, but I'm not satisfied offering her the life of a farmer's wife." He bridled his horse and fastened the straps. "I'm going over to see if Elijah Carr's offer still stands." He turned to look at his aunt, and he was surprised by the uncertainty in her eyes. "You think I shouldn't? You were the one telling me he would give me a good price."

"Yes, I know," she slowly replied. "At first I thought you were keeping the farm because of your pa, but I've come to realize the reason is much different than that. And much more important. Are you sure you want to do this?"

"Yes," he said. He pulled himself up into the saddle and looked down at his aunt. "Don't tell Katherine. I. . .I want to surprise her." But as he rode off, he struggled to ignore the growing feeling of doubt in his heart.

eighteen

"Katherine, did you hear what I said?"

Katherine started at Mary's question and turned away from the window. She, Adele, and Mary had been carefully piecing together quilt blocks, and they now had enough for a good-sized quilt. Some of them were laid out on the table in the dining room to see how they would look once they were all pieced together. Once the top was done they would invite Ruth, May, and Mrs. Warren over to help quilt it. But Katherine's heart wasn't in it. She was too worried about Daniel.

Just a little while ago, for the second time in two weeks, Daniel had ridden off on Scioto with Mr. O'Conner following in his buggy. It couldn't be money related. Even during the war the farm had done well, and in spite of how it had looked when they had returned, Elijah Carr had not shirked in keeping the animals and fields well cared for.

But Daniel had been distracted and moody ever since he'd left her sitting in the parlor. At first she'd been concerned that he was having trouble with his memories of the war, but Michael had assured her he hadn't talked to him about it since her brother left.

She bit her lip and looked down at the quilt blocks on the table. Plucking one up, she looked at it absentmindedly.

"We can assume you don't like it," Mary said.

Katherine looked at her and then back down at the table. "Oh I'm sorry, Mary," she said, replacing the block and looking at them. Mary had let her decide the pattern, and she had settled on an Irish chain. "It looks beautiful, but I wonder if we should have done it on point," she said, referring to the way they could have pieced the blocks so that the squares were sitting on one point, making them look like diamonds.

"That would have been very pretty," Adele said, looking at the squares. "But I like the way this looks just as well. Perhaps next time we will do as you suggest and we can use some appliqué. I will show you how."

When it had been decided that Adele and Jacob would continue staying at the Kirby farm, Adele brought over a quilt her grandmother had made when she had lived in Zoar. It was an orange-and-green floral appliquéd pattern on a white background, and Katherine had admired the careful workmanship.

Suddenly the wind whipped up and blew the squares on top of one another. Adele and Katherine gathered them up while Mary went to the window. "A storm's blowing in," she said, shutting the window. "I hope Daniel and Mr. O'Conner stay safe."

"Mary, just where were they going?" Katherine asked. Surely she knew something about what her nephew was up to.

"Daniel asked us not to say anything," Mary said quietly. "It's nothing to fret over."

"Then why would he tell you not to tell me?" If Katherine had been worried about Daniel before, she was twice so now. Adele and Mary looked at each other and Katherine frowned. "What's going on?"

"Do you want some tea, dear?" Mary asked, trying to avoid her question.

But Katherine wasn't about to be put off. "Mary, I want to know what Daniel's doing."

"We should tell her, Mary," Adele said quietly.

Mary grasped Katherine's hands. "Daniel's decided to sell the farm to Elijah Carr. He's on his way to his farm now to sign the papers."

Katherine stared at them before walking out into the hall and taking her bonnet from its peg. Adele and Mary followed her and stood in the doorway. She quickly tied on her bonnet and grabbed a shawl.

"Where on earth are you going?" Mary exclaimed as she opened the door. The sky was dark and the wind was whipping the trees back and forth furiously.

"I'm going to stop him," she declared and ran out the door before they could stop her.

The rain began to fall in heavy drops by the time she reached the end of the drive, and she covered her head with the shawl. It all made sense now, his mood, the meetings with Mr. O'Conner. He was selling the land and he wasn't happy about it. And the only reason he wouldn't was if he knew he was going against the Lord's will.

The thought caused her to move faster and she began to run. But soon her skirts and petticoats were waterlogged, and she was forced to go far slower than she would have liked. Thunder shook the very air around her, and she turned to see black clouds rolling in from the west. Her heart began to pound with fear, but she hurried on, determined to keep Daniel from going against God's will.

She had just rounded a slight curve in the road when she caught sight of a horse and rider galloping toward her. It was Daniel. She was too late.

Catching sight of her, he brought Scioto to a sudden halt and the horse danced in a small circle as he spoke. "Katherine, what are you doing here?" he yelled over the rain and thunder. "Are you crazy?"

"Daniel Aaron Kirby, how could you!" she yelled back. She was so angry she failed to notice the wind was becoming fiercer. "What do you mean by selling the farm?"

Daniel didn't answer. He took one look at the western sky

and, grabbing Katherine by the wrist, hauled her up behind him in the saddle. Before she could utter a word of protest, Scioto was off like a shot and she clung to Daniel for dear life.

All at once they were back at the farm. As she slid from the saddle she heard a low distant rumble like that of a train. Daniel heard it, too, and after jumping down, he gave his horse a solid swat on the hindquarters before grabbing Katherine's hand and running for the root cellar.

&

Daniel swung her inside and shut the door tight behind them. He hoped Simon Peter had been able to get his aunt, Adele, and Jacob into the secret room out in the barn. It was the safest place on the farm during a tornado. He would have taken Katherine there, too, but he could tell by the sound of the storm they wouldn't have made it there in time. Daniel fumbled for the lantern that was kept on one of the shelves and lit it. Turning around he realized he might as well have shut himself up with an angry bobcat.

Katherine stood there with her arms crossed, soaking wet and positively livid. She had every right to be angry, of course. He was angry at himself for even considering. . .

The wind suddenly took on an awful low squeal, and although it wasn't as close as it had been before, now was not the time to discuss the matter. He pulled her down next to him against the back wall where the cellar was nestled into the side of a small hill. It would give them the best protection if the tornado hit the farm.

Katherine seemed to realize what was happening and didn't resist. Much. For a few tense seconds, Daniel wasn't sure anything would be left standing, but the low rumble seemed to go further north and he began to relax as the winds eased a little.

"I think we're safe for now," he finally said.

"Good," Katherine declared as she jumped to her feet. "I'm

not spending one more second cooped up in here with you."
She started for the door but Daniel grabbed her arm. She tried
to yank it away. "Let me go!"

"No, there might be more," he snapped, and to prove his
point the winds slammed into the tiny building, making it
shake. "Aren't there tornados in South Carolina?"

"Yes, but the *hurricanes* there are worse," she shot back.
Apparently he was just about to encounter one since she gave
him a stinging slap on the arm which hurt twice as much since
his shirt was soaking wet.

"Ow! Wait, Kath—"

"How could you?" She started to lay into him again, but he
grabbed her arm. "Let go!"

"Katherine, I didn't sell the farm."

She stopped struggling and stared at him. "What?"

He pulled her close. "I didn't sell the farm. I couldn't. I got
all the way to Elijah Carr's drive today, but in the end God
wouldn't let me."

The last two weeks had been the worst of Daniel's life. The
whole process had been difficult, as if the Lord had been
giving him time to reconsider. He and Carr had been unable
to decide on a price, and then business had kept Mr. O'Conner
from getting the papers drawn up right away. When he had
approached Dr. Harris, his old mentor had tried to talk him
out of selling the farm, in spite of how eager he'd always been
for Daniel to become a professor. And the distinct feeling
that he was going against God's will was next to impossible
to ignore.

Katherine spoke, rousing him from his thoughts. "Daniel,
why ever did you consider such a thing?"

"For you," he whispered. He saw the confusion in her face
and continued. "I didn't want to be a farmer when I gave you
this." He pulled the ring from his pocket, laying it in her small

hand. "This has been in my family since before the Kirbys came to America. My grandfather gave it to my grandmother, and Pa gave it to Ma." His heart pounded as wonder and joy softly spread over her delicate little face. "Marry me?"

She answered him with a long, slow kiss.

"I'm sorry," he said a moment later. "You deserve much better than a farmer. I—"

Katherine laid her fingers over his lips and smiled. "I *am* getting better than a farmer. Much better. I'm getting you."

⁊ₐ

Katherine watched from the parlor window as Daniel strode back to the house with Simon Peter and his sons, the last bit of sunlight drifting from the evening sky. It had taken them the rest of the afternoon to round up the livestock and see what kind of damage the tornado had caused.

They had been lucky. Apparently the tornado had tracked north, skipping nearly all of their land. There was only minor damage to the barn and a couple of the outbuildings and only two fields would need to be replanted. Daniel had been grateful there had been no hail.

Everything had been accounted for. Except Scioto. Daniel's horse couldn't be found anywhere.

Stepping outside, Katherine joined Daniel as he said good-bye to Simon Peter, Michael, and Aaron.

"We'll keep our eyes open while we're riding back home," Simon said as he took up the reins. "If we find him, I'll send him on home with Michael."

"Thanks," Daniel said gloomily.

"Don't you worry," Michael said. "Jeremiah said he's never seen such a smart horse. He'll be back." The young man reached out and gave Daniel a quick hug and a slap on the back before climbing into his pa's wagon.

Katherine waved as they drove off and then turned to

Daniel. "We'll find him," she said softly as he pulled her into a quick embrace. "He'll probably be standing outside the barn door come morning."

"I hope so," he said.

Stepping inside the house, they went into the parlor. Katherine immediately went over to the secretary where they kept the books they were discussing. "What shall we talk about tonight?"

"I hope it's not that Sissy man again tonight," Jacob said as he played on the floor with Toby's old lead soldier set.

Adele looked at her son from where she sat on the sofa with Mary as they sewed. "Mein *dummer*, Junge." She chuckled. "What do you mean?"

"I'm not a silly boy," Jacob said defensively. He looked at Daniel who sat in the high-backed easy chair. "You know, Sissyroo, Sis. . .sis. . ."

"You mean Cicero?" Daniel asked and laughed when the boy nodded.

Katherine was grateful Jacob had taken Daniel's mind off his lost horse even if only for a moment.

"I think I'll just read to us from one of the Psalms tonight."

Katherine brought him his Bible, and he kissed her hand before she went to sit between Mary and Adele.

"All right, you two," Mary said reproachfully then smiled. "Well, I guess I can't be too hard on you. John and I were just as quick to steal a kiss as anyone else."

"Nathaniel was the same," Adele said softly. She was silent for a moment before smiling playfully. "But Nathaniel did not propose to me in a root cellar."

"Well, I didn't exactly plan it that way."

Katherine looked at Daniel and watched as his cheeks reddened for a change. "I think it was lovely," she declared, looking at him.

His soft green eyes glowed with gratitude.

"Well, I wish I had been in the root cellar instead of the barn," Jacob said. Simon Peter had hustled everyone into the secret room Daniel had been sleeping in after making sure the livestock had been set loose. The young boy hadn't liked going down into the closed-in space in spite of the fact they'd had two lanterns.

"Better there than out in the storm," Mary said. She glanced at Katherine and Daniel. "You two were lucky you weren't blown off the face of the earth."

Daniel frowned and Katherine knew he was thinking about Scioto again. "Where did you and Simon Peter and the boys look this afternoon?" she asked.

"We didn't have enough light to look very far," he said thoughtfully. "I wish I had seen which direction he had gone. I'm going to go looking for him after church tomorrow."

"I'll come with you," Katherine said.

"Jacob and I could use some exercise so we will come, too." Adele smiled as her son gave a little whoop and thanked her. "Four sets of eyes are better than two. Do you want to come with us, Mary?"

"Well, I don't know about me," she replied. Her foot, while mostly healed, was still a little tender. "I think I'll stay behind and read my Bible."

Adele, Katherine, and Daniel looked at each other with knowing smiles. Mary might start out reading her Bible, but she would end up taking a Sunday afternoon nap. But she more than made up for it as she usually read every night before going to bed.

"Well, Jacob," Daniel said as he opened his Bible, "since we bored you with Cicero for the past few nights, what Psalm should I read?"

"Can we read a story instead?" the boy asked hopefully,

"about Elijah and the prophets of Baal?"

As Daniel turned to First Kings, Katherine took up her sewing and caught the glint of gold on her right hand. Her heart jumped as she glanced at the ring Daniel had given her. Mary said she remembered her sister wearing the band on her right ring finger after Joseph had proposed to her, and Katherine eagerly did the same.

She glanced up at Daniel who was now reading to a very attentive Jacob. He'd noticed what she'd done at dinner and had smiled with approval. Daniel intended that she be a fall bride. When the leaves would be just beginning to match her eyes, he'd said.

Katherine bit her lip and smiled. She hadn't been able to understand at first what was so different about her appearance when she looked in the mirror over the past couple of weeks. Then she finally understood she was seeing herself through Daniel's eyes and the love he had for her. She started in on her sewing with a contented smile.

"I will praise thee, O Lord, with my whole heart."

nineteen

Unfortunately Scioto was not standing outside the barn door or anywhere else about the farm by the next morning.

After services, Daniel decided the best way to look would be east of the farm. "He would have been trying to head away from the storm once I let him go," he reasoned.

After lunch he, Adele, Jacob, and Katherine set out over the fields. Daniel grasped Katherine's hand and he showed her what fields had been planted and which fields were laying fallow for the season. But he was clearly distracted, and Katherine knew he was worried about his horse. She glanced at his belt. He'd brought his Colt with him. She just hoped if they did find the animal he wouldn't have to use it.

"Where did you get Scioto?" she eventually asked.

"He found me." Daniel stopped for a moment and scanned the horizon. The only things in view were a line of trees and Adele and Jacob walking several feet away to their left. "I'd gotten nicked in the leg by a bullet," he said as they continued walking. "I was lost in some woods, and I wasn't sure if I was behind enemy lines or not. My horse had been shot out from under me. Then I heard movement in the brush nearby and there he was, large as life, urging me to get up. I managed to swing myself up and he just took off. I was back with my regiment before I knew it." He sighed and looked over the horizon once more. "As swift and sure as the Scioto River. That's how he got his name."

Katherine squeezed his hand. "We'll find him. I'm sure of it."

"Thank you, Kat." He kissed her on the forehead.

Katherine was about to ask him why he was suddenly

calling her Kat when Adele called out to them. They quickly made their way over to her and Jacob.

"Mr. Kirby, I found hoofprints!" the boy said excitedly.

"They probably belong to our plow horses," he said as he knelt down to examine the prints. "No, these can't belong to Belle and Babe."

"Why not?" Katherine asked.

"They're too small for one, and there's only one set of them."

"Then these might belong to Scioto?" Adele asked.

"Yes," Daniel muttered and started walking in the same direction as the prints. Katherine, Adele, and Jacob followed. The tracks stopped just before the fence that marked the edge of the Kirby property and continued on the other side.

"This is Elijah Carr's property," Adele said. Her face tensed slightly. "At least it is now."

"Adele?" Katherine laid a gentle hand on her arm and the woman clasped it.

"This land used to belong to her and Nate," Daniel said quietly. "Jacob and I could go on. Let Kat take you back to the house."

Adele looked out over the fields for a moment. "No, I will be all right."

Daniel started to climb the fence but Katherine was hesitant, remembering how Carr had chased Jacob off his land a few weeks ago. "Do you think we should?"

"While I was out with Simon Peter we met up with one of Carr's farmhands chasing after a stray cow. He said we could look if we needed to."

Once they were over the fence Katherine walked on with Adele. "Our house was over that way," Adele said, pointing to the line of trees. Katherine caught sight of a slate roof.

The field they were walking over was lying fallow, and they lost the prints in the tall weeds and grass that had grown in it. They spread out hoping to find them again, and Katherine thought it would be worth taking a peek at the farmhouse.

Brush and young trees had grown up around it, and she pushed her way through until she came to a sort of clearing. The house stood before her. It was a small frame house and as Jacob had said, the glass windows were broken out. A pump stood nearby, and she could imagine Adele pumping water from it to get Jacob or Nate something to drink. Her heart ached for her friend's loss.

"Father," she whispered, "help Adele find happiness again." Katherine had noticed how wistfully the young widow would look at her and Daniel. She knew no one could ever replace Nate in the young widow's heart, but she believed the Lord could bless her with room for another. And then Jacob could have a pa again.

Suddenly a familiar face appeared around the corner of the house.

"Scioto," Katherine exclaimed softly.

The horse grunted as she approached, and she gathered the reins which hung broken from his bit. She led him out further into the clearing, pleased to see he seemed perfectly sound. She made certain by leading him around in a circle before bringing him to a stop. She rubbed his neck and he nuzzled her. "We've been worried sick about you, boy," she murmured.

She stiffened as she heard the click of a gun being cocked. She turned to see Charles step out of the trees.

"And I have been just as concerned for you, sister dear," he said as he leveled the gun at her.

"Charles!" she gasped.

"I'm glad to see there was no permanent damage done." He was referring to the blow he had dealt her, and she raised a hand to her face. "It's just too bad I didn't knock some sense into you."

"What are you still doing here? Where did you get the gun?"

"As I told you before, you will do as I say. We're going to leave for home right now on that horse, so lead him over."

Katherine turned and in one swift movement slapped Scioto on the hindquarters. The horse screamed and took off running toward the fields. "Daniel!" she yelled as Charles grabbed her and threw his hand over her mouth.

"What'd you do a fool thing like that for?"

"It's a good thing she did, secesh." Elijah Carr rushed out of the trees, a shotgun in hand. "You were planning on walking out on our deal. She still has to get Kirby over here, remember?"

Charles scowled at the older man. "Well, you heard the man, sister dear," he growled as he dug his gun painfully into her ribs. "Call him again."

෨

Daniel saw Scioto burst out of the brush at the same moment he heard Katherine calling for him. He knew instantly something was wrong. His horse came to a stop before him. Had Scioto hurt her somehow?

Adele and Jacob rushed up as Katherine called for him again. She sounded frightened, and Daniel drew his Colt.

"Daniel, what is it?" Adele asked.

"Something's wrong," he said. "Take Scioto and get help."

Without hesitation she swung herself up into the saddle, and Daniel helped Jacob climb up in front of her. As they galloped off he jogged toward Nate's old house, slowing as he drew close.

He reached the clearing and saw Charles standing near the house with a gun pointed at Katherine's head. "Katherine!"

"Now, now, she'll be just fine as long as you do as I say."

Daniel felt the muzzle of a shotgun in his ribs and he instantly uncocked his weapon and let go of the grip so it hung from his finger.

Elijah Carr took it and, sticking it in his belt, nudged him toward a large stump where a pen and inkpot sat. "We're just going to conduct a little business."

Daniel watched as Carr walked around him and laid the sale papers on the stump. "Where did those come from? They should still be with Mr. O'Conner."

"Mr. O'Conner had to stay with me for a while until the storm blew over." He smiled meanly. "One of my hands managed to get ahold of these for me." He nodded toward the papers. "Now sign."

Daniel looked at Katherine and then back at Carr. There was no way around it. If he didn't do what Carr asked, either he or Charles would shoot Katherine, more than likely killing her. His heart pounded and he knelt down, picked up the pen, and dipped it in the ink.

He was about to sign his name when Katherine spoke. "Mr. Carr, all the land in the world won't bring your brother back," she said softly.

Carr stared at her. "What do you know about my brother, secesh?"

"I know he died a horrible death at the hands of foolish men. I've been praying for your nephew and your sister-in-law. And for you."

Something hit Daniel's boot. Carr's attention was diverted, and Daniel slowly looked down to see a buckeye lying at the base of the stump. He stared at it in amazement, not because it was nowhere near the season for the nuts to fall but because of the letters he saw etched in it. J. M. K. Jonah Michael Kirby. Praying that he was not imagining things, he laid the pen down and rose.

Carr looked at him then noticed the unsigned papers. "What do you think you're doing?"

"We've all been praying for you, Elijah," he replied. "Even Adele. Even me."

A look of amazement fell over Carr's face, much to Daniel's surprise. He didn't know the man's face could look anything but greedy and hateful. His mother had been right. He should have been praying for the man all along.

"Mr. Carr, I—" Katherine began. She winced as Charles roughly grabbed her arm.

Daniel had to fight the urge not to do something stupid.

"My sister is obviously disturbing you, sir," he said. "So we'll be on our way."

Carr's face resumed its normal expression. "Just what makes you think you're free to leave?"

"It was part of the deal," Charles snapped.

"I don't deal with Johnny Rebs," Carr replied, turning his shotgun toward the pair.

Katherine screamed as Charles shot Elijah Carr in the chest. The man fell to the ground and Daniel dove for his gun. He pulled it from Carr's belt, but Charles rushed up and kicked it out of his hand.

"Your turn now, Billy Yank," Charles sneered, aiming right at Daniel's head.

A shot rang out and Charles slumped to the ground next to Carr. Daniel heard Katherine gasp as his own brother stepped from the bushes.

Jonah looked at him. "Guess it was his turn."

twenty

The babble of Mill Creek filled Katherine's ears as she sank down on a rock by the water's edge. She breathed deeply and looked out over her peaceful surroundings, but her hands were still shaky and she still could not quite believe what had happened. Her brother was dead, and Elijah Carr had only survived long enough to die in his own bed.

When Charles had left the Kirby farm, he had wandered onto Elijah Carr's land and found the Stephenses' old farmhouse. According to one of Carr's farmhands, he'd been staying there for the past two weeks before being discovered the day of the storm. When Carr questioned him, he realized he could use him to get Daniel to sign the sale papers.

She began to shake as the whole episode played out in her head once more. If it hadn't been for Jonah, Daniel would be dead right now, and she would be getting dragged back to South Carolina to be forced into a loveless marriage.

She shook her head. Like everyone else, she still couldn't quite believe Daniel's older brother was alive.

Like Charles, Jonah had been reported as being killed in action. But in reality, he'd been sent to a Confederate prisoner-of-war camp, none other than the notorious Andersonville Prison. Jonah had barely survived the harsh conditions and had been forced to watch helplessly as many of his fellow prisoners died of exposure and malnutrition.

When he was finally released, the army had put him and many other prisoners from Ohio on the steamship *Sultana*. The hopelessly overcrowded riverboat trudged up the Mississippi

River and was just a few miles north of Memphis, Tennessee when it exploded. Jonah had been able to jump from the ship and swim to safety, but he became ill and had to stay in a Memphis hospital for several days before finally arriving home. He'd literally just walked up the drive when Adele had come charging up on Scioto.

Father, Your timing is perfect. Thank You for protecting us.

She heard footsteps and turned to see Daniel stepping into the shadow of the trees. He gave her a little smile. "Thought I might find you here." He walked over and sat down next to her on the rock, slipping his arm around her.

She rested her head against his shoulder. "I needed a little peace and quiet. What did the sheriff say?"

"He said Jonah only did what he had to do to defend me. When he searched Carr's papers he found his will. The land will go to his nephew, Ben."

"Does the sheriff know how to reach him?"

Daniel nodded. "He found a number of letters from Carr's sister-in-law and from Ben. It'll take a while to reach them. They're clear out in the far western part of the Dakota Territory." He squeezed her. "What do you plan to do about your brother?"

She sighed. "I'll telegraph Aunt Ada. Most likely she'll have me bury him here. She won't want to have to tell Charleston society what happened." She brushed a tear from her eye and felt Daniel squeeze her shoulder. "I had hoped Charles would have a chance to change his heart before he died."

"I'm sorry," Daniel said.

Katherine laid her head back on his broad shoulder, and they looked out at the soothing waters of Mill Creek.

After a while she raised her head. "How's Jonah?"

Daniel paused for a moment and Katherine knew he, too, was finding it hard to believe his brother was alive. "Adele went with him just now to see Ma's grave." He sighed. "He's not very happy with me, though." He rose and walked up to the edge of the creek. "I'm not very happy with myself. I came very close—too close—to throwing away his inheritance. I should have trusted what the Lord was telling me."

Katherine joined him and took his hand in both of hers. " 'If we confess our sins, he is faithful and just to forgive us our sins, and to cleanse us from all unrighteousness.' God will forgive you, and I know Jonah will in time."

He smiled at her tenderly, reaching up with his free hand to stroke her face. "Thank you, Kat."

She looked at him curiously. "That's the third time you've called me that today."

"It's to remind me never to get you angry." He pulled her into his arms. "You get as feisty as a wild bobcat."

"Are you sure you can love such a dangerous creature?" she teased him. She caught her breath at the look in his eyes.

He lowered his head and kissed her until everything around her spun. "Katherine Eliza Wallace, I'll love you until Mill Creek runs dry, and forever after that."

epilogue

"Now what God hath joined together, let no man put asunder," Rev. Warren declared. He smiled at Daniel. "You may now kiss the bride."

Katherine laid her hands lightly on her new husband's chest as he tenderly kissed her.

A soft sigh of approval rose from all those assembled in the Kirby parlor. No sooner had the reverend presented them as Mr. and Mrs. Daniel Kirby than it seemed the entire crowd moved forward as one to wish them well. With embraces and handshakes, one person after another congratulated the happy pair and Katherine thought her arms would fall off before they were through.

Jonah stepped forward and, nodding to her, soberly shook his brother's hand. "I'm happy for both of you," he said and, without so much as smiling at them, stepped away.

Katherine looked at Daniel and he squeezed her hand in reassurance.

Mary stepped up and hugged her and her nephew.

"I pray he'll be all right," Katherine said as they parted.

Mary looked after Jonah with weary eyes. "He needs all the prayers he can get right now."

"Is he still having nightmares?" Daniel asked.

"I'm afraid so," she replied.

Jonah walked into the empty dining room and was soon followed by Adele. She laid a hand on his arm, and the hard look left his face for a moment.

"He seems a little better when she's around, though," Mary added.

Adele and Jacob were staying with the Deckers, but the young widow came out to the Kirby farm nearly every day to help Mary.

"A soothing presence," Daniel said, looking at his new bride. He looked around the room before turning back and smiling at her, a spark in his green eyes. "Mary, Katherine, come here. I have a little surprise."

"Daniel Aaron Kirby, what else have you done?" Katherine asked as she lifted the full skirts of her new dress. It was made of cream-colored linen which Ruth Decker had special ordered just for Katherine. With Jonah having taken over the farm, Daniel had accepted the position as a classics professor at Ohio Wesleyan alongside Professor Harris. He'd already surprised her with their new house in Delaware and news that they would honeymoon in Maine. He also promised they would visit with his good friend General Joshua Chamberlain and his family while they were there. How could there possibly be more?

She and Mary looked at each other in confusion as Daniel led them over to where the Johnson clan stood. It had been months since they had seen Simon Peter and his sons. Jonah had taken over what was left of the planting when he came home, and they had been busy out at their own farm.

With a broad smile, Simon Peter took her hand in his. "How do, Mrs. Kirby," he said. "Things been so busy you haven't met my wife Celia yet."

"I'm so glad to meet you," Celia said, clasping Katherine's hands. The woman smiled at Daniel and then looked back at her. "Mrs. Kirby, I believe you already know my sister."

Wondering what she could mean, Katherine looked to see a young woman step out from behind Simon Peter's tall form. "Katherine, I'm so very glad for you."

"Chloe!" Katherine and Mary both gasped and they quickly embraced her.

Katherine held her at arm's length, her eyes swimming with tears. "Oh Chloe, I'm so sorry—"

"Oh no, Katherine, don't blame yourself. I never did." The two of them embraced tightly once more.

Katherine looked at Daniel. "How long have you known she was Celia's sister?"

"A while," he admitted. "I wanted to tell you right away, but Chloe wanted to surprise you."

As the guests began to slowly leave, Katherine stepped out into the courtyard for some fresh air and to breathe a quick prayer of thanks. October was starting out a bit chilly and she shivered.

A moment later she found herself being wrapped in something warm. Looking down, she saw her Irish chain quilt that Mary and Adele had lovingly finished in time for her wedding day. Daniel's strong arms soon followed and she leaned back against his chest as they watched the sun slowly dip lower over the fields.

With a sigh of contentment, she turned her head slightly to glance back at her husband and he turned her in his arms and kissed her with a passion that rivaled the horizon's fiery glow.

"How ever did I manage it?" Katherine eventually murmured.

"Manage what?" Daniel smiled.

"How did I, of all people, manage to capture a Yankee heart?"

A Letter To Our Readers

Dear Reader:

In order that we might better contribute to your reading enjoyment, we would appreciate your taking a few minutes to respond to the following questions. We welcome your comments and read each form and letter we receive. When completed, please return to the following:

Fiction Editor
Heartsong Presents
PO Box 719
Uhrichsville, Ohio 44683

1. Did you enjoy reading *Yankee Heart* by Jennifer A. Davids?
   ❏ Very much! I would like to see more books by this author!
   ❏ Moderately. I would have enjoyed it more if

   _____

   _____

   _____

2. Are you a member of **Heartsong Presents**? ❏ Yes ❏ No
   If no, where did you purchase this book? _____

   _____

3. How would you rate, on a scale from 1 (poor) to 5 (superior), the cover design? _____

4. On a scale from 1 (poor) to 10 (superior), please rate the following elements.

   ____ Heroine   ____ Plot
   ____ Hero   ____ Inspirational theme
   ____ Setting   ____ Secondary characters

5. These characters were special because? _____
_____
_____

6. How has this book inspired your life? _____
_____
_____

7. What settings would you like to see covered in future
   Heartsong Presents books? _____
_____
_____

8. What are some inspirational themes you would like to see
   treated in future books? _____
_____
_____

9. Would you be interested in reading other **Heartsong
   Presents** titles? ❏ Yes   ❏ No

10. Please check your age range:
        ❏ Under 18   ❏ 18-24
        ❏ 25-34   ❏ 35-45
        ❏ 46-55   ❏ Over 55

Name _____
Occupation _____
Address _____
City, State, Zip _____
E-mail _____

Heart♥ong

Presents

Great Inspirational Romance at a Great Price!

Heartsong Presents books are inspirational romances in contemporary and historical settings, designed to give you an enjoyable, spirit-lifting reading experience. You can choose wonderfully written titles from some of today's best authors like Wanda E. Brunstetter, Mary Connealy, Susan Page Davis, Cathy Marie Hake, Joyce Livingston, and many others.

When ordering quantities less than six, above titles are $3.99 each.
Not all titles may be available at time of order.

SEND TO: **Heartsong Presents** Readers' Service
P.O. Box 721, Uhrichsville, Ohio 44683

Please send me the items checked above. I am enclosing $ _____
(please add $4.00 to cover postage per order. OH add 7% tax. WA add 8.5%). Send check or money order, no cash or C.O.D.s, please.
To place a credit card order, call 1-740-922-7280.

NAME _____

ADDRESS _____

CITY/STATE _____ ZIP_____

HPS 7-11

HEARTSONG
PRESENTS

If you love Christian romance...

$12.⁹⁹

You'll love Heartsong Presents' inspiring and faith-filled romances by today's very best Christian authors...Wanda E. Brunstetter, Mary Connealy, Susan Page Davis, Cathy Marie Hake, and Joyce Livingston, to mention a few!

When you join Heartsong Presents, you'll enjoy four brand-new, mass-market, 176-page books—two contemporary and two historical—that will build you up in your faith when you discover God's role in every relationship you read about!

Mass Market 176 Pages

Imagine...four new romances every four weeks—with men and women like you who long to meet the one God has chosen as the love of their lives...all for the low price of $12.99 postpaid.

To join, simply visit www.heartsong presents.com or complete the coupon below and mail it to the address provided.

✂ -

YES! Sign me up for Heart♥ng!

**NEW MEMBERSHIPS WILL BE SHIPPED IMMEDIATELY!
Send no money now.** We'll bill you only $12.99 postpaid with your first shipment of four books. Or for faster action, call 1-740-922-7280.

NAME_____

ADDRESS_____

CITY_____ STATE _____ ZIP _____

**MAIL TO: HEARTSONG PRESENTS, P.O. Box 721, Uhrichsville, Ohio 44683
or sign up at WWW.HEARTSONGPRESENTS.COM**